MEMOIRS FROM THE ASYLUM

KENNETH WEENE

ALL THINGS THAT MATTER PRESS

MEMOIRS FROM THE ASYLUM

ISBN: 978-0-9844219-5-4

Library of Congress Control Number: 2010904952

Author Photo by Roz Weene

Cover Design by All Things That Matter Press

Printed in 2010 by All Things That Matter Press

CHAPTER ONE

I should have started earlier. I'm too old, and it's too damn late. I wish that I could blame someone else for my mistake. There were lots of people who told me it would be a stupid decision – that there was much of life for me to explore, possibly even to conquer; but I chose to not listen. Why? Because I was scared. Pure and simple, I'm a coward. Life had too many potential pitfalls, and I have always wanted to play it safe.

Other guys went to Vietnam after college. Hell, some even left school and volunteered. I didn't think it was a good war, but that was only the secondary reason for avoiding the service. I was scared, terrified. I didn't want to die, but more – I didn't want to hurt. Pain scares the crap out of me. I don't do pain – never did and never will.

Then, too, I was scared of trying things that I couldn't do. I'm one of those people who rehearse for getting up in the morning. I go through the sequence: what I'm going to wear, which tasks I'm going to complete, even what I'm going to think about. If something seems too difficult, screw it. If there's a bunch of too difficult things on the roster, well, screw the whole day; I stay in my bed – my safe, unchallenging bed. With my face turned to the wall and my knees hugged securely to my breast, I journey inward – to the safety of my within.

There was a period, back in the early sixties, when I often stayed in bed for days on end just getting up to shit and to graze out of my refrigerator. Usually it was the need for new supplies – the realization that what remained of my grazing space had slowly grown the green beard of time – that got me up for a couple of days.

Eventually, I'd hit Sloame's for some groceries. Then, bologna, bread, soda, cheese – and mustard, mustn't forget the mustard: all in fridge, and back to bed I'd go.

Safety is a relative thing. In the bigger picture, my life went from bad to worse. But, I wasn't in 'Nam. I wasn't failing at a job. I wasn't getting into trouble with people. I was simply being schizophrenic. Disbilitied, Social Securitied, and indulged by parents hiding their loathing and frustration. Being schizophrenic isn't so bad – at least not until they, the great unspecified they that is society, say screw it, screw you, and lock you away in the warehouse of unliving dementia.

Those dingy green-yellow hospital walls are really off-putting. It's like living inside a puddle of puke. The people are the chunks of undigested food – no longer human, just unidentified floating objects.

Some of them are really revolting. The others, "the patients," aren't so bad.

Mostly, the diagnosed only want to be left alone – alone – caught between the grief of being and the terror of not. Once in a while there'll be somebody who wants to fight the world, but mostly the world they want to fight is that revolting staff, so you silently root them on. At least, that is how I see it.

Charlie wants to rape the nurse's aide; good for Charlie. The nurse's aide is twice Charlie's size and has a right like Muhammad Ali; too bad for Charlie. Charlie ends up with an ass full of Valium; good for him. They lock Charlie on the violent ward – who the hell was Charlie?

Charlie comes back to the ward; good for Charlie. He's had enough shock to fry his brain; too bad for Charlie. He shuffles along and drools; when he's excited he shouts "Oh, boy!" in a repetitive Tourette bark – now Charlie fits in. Good for Charlie? Nope, good for the system. Modern medicine has won another round. The world of the asylum grinds the people; it makes pabulum of their brains and mush of their wills. The system works; the person doesn't. We all celebrate Charlie's return by standing around and rocking from side to side.

Some of us stare at the television. There's a soap opera on. The picture rolls. Nobody seems to notice. Certainly, nobody cares. Most of our minds are rolling, too. Half the staring patients are watching their own programs, the ones in their heads. Vertical hold is not a strong point among the crazy.

Jack wants to take over the world. He plans on leading a revolution; he plans to start in Australia. He stares at the television and sees troop movements. In his program, he is leading an army. He is riding on a large black horse and is dressed in fatigues. He carries a magic sword. A bit anachronistic, but what the hell, it's his program. It doesn't matter; he's too doped on phenothiazines to walk across the room without being told. Instead he pill-rolls his fingers and shakes. They're supposed to give out Cogentin for the Parkinsons, but the nurses don't bother. Instead one of them sells the bottles in town. It doesn't bring much, but they save up for their Fourth of July party. They could get more for other drugs. Valium is good on the streets, but they don't get much extra; they're too busy shoving it into us. Mostly they just unload Cogentin and some antibiotics. It buys them a case of beer to commemorate their freedom, to celebrate the all-important fact that they have the keys.

Sue is writhing against the wall. She's in a jacket. The arms are tied behind her. Eventually she'll work her way out. She always does. Then she'll take off her clothes and try to get laid. One of the aides will drag her protesting to the rubber room. Most of the time she ends up frustrated; but if pimple-faced Harry is on duty, he'll give her what she wants. They'll couple quickly on the rubberized floor. Everybody knows what he's doing. Everybody makes believe they don't. Besides which, nobody cares,

Harry got her pregnant three months ago. She had a quick D and C. No baby, no foul. Harry strutted around looking pleased as a shark in a school of haddock. Way to go, Harry. You can impregnate a helpless nut job. Way to go, state hospital. You can cover things up without missing a beat. Way to go, Sue. You can attract a no-brained prick. Is everybody happy?

I'm not. I'm safe, but I sure ain't happy. Life's a trade-off. Isn't that what they say?

Mitch is throwing stuff at the TV. There isn't much to throw in this day room: a few books that have browned and greased with age, bits and pieces of board games that nobody ever played, decks of cards – mostly recreated from lots of other decks until the backs are as distinctive as the faces – and half-ripped magazines that the aides bring to read during their shifts and then leave scattered around. Mitch wanders around picking up this debris and heaving it at the television. Only a couple of the books hit their mark. The picture goes on rolling. Two aides and a nurse wrestle Mitch to the floor and pull down the back of his pants. The nurse inserts her Valium phallus into his butt. Soon he won't remember why he was throwing anything. They wait until he's nodding off and then half drag him to his bed where he's safely lashed down. As they're tying him in place, one of the aides will get his jollies with a quick punch to the gut. Nobody will object, not unless you count Mitch's wordless grunt. Nobody counts grunts around here.

Alzheimer's has Mitch. Every now and then it gets him restless, and he blows like an old geyser that's running out of steam. The rest of the time he wanders around talking to himself. They say that he was once a college professor. So, it isn't really that different; he's just talking to himself in a new place. Guess what? Nobody cares.

Mitch never married. He has nobody to take care of him. One of his cousins, his closest living relative from among a collection of the uncaring, had him committed. Now he has the state – the state as parent – the great father – the great white father. Hell, now I sound hebephrenic.

These damn yellow-green puke walls get to me. The mismatched clothes pulled from the laundry and haphazardly distributed among us helpless inmates get to me. The rolling television screen gets to me. The metal screens on the window get to me. The ugly, nasty staff gets to me. The pointlessness of the people gets to me. The pointlessness of me gets to me.

This wasn't the plan. I was supposed to become a businessman. That's what I went to school for. That's what I had intended, getting rich screwing the world. Then I got scared. Of course, now the army won't want me. I could leave the hospital and resume my life. I could. I could except that I'm still scared.

What am I so scared of? What fills life with terror for me while other guys go about living with no problem? The doctors come and go here. Each one gives out new diagnoses, new explanations, and new medications. The residents try to talk with us. They have ward meetings and talk about the things like their arrivals and departures, things that they think are affecting us. They don't realize that nothing much affects any of us; we're all pretty well beyond the petty shit of this world. We live in our own distorted, phenothiazines laced, no-fears-here, Nirvana.

***

Before, when I was still out there, I talked to a couple of shrinks. I told them early memories. I looked at loony inkblots and made them into monsters and vampires: I dripped blood from vampire fangs, swam in fire, and drowned in their ocean of fiends.

I looked at pictures from long-ago America and made up stories. One, the one that disturbed me the most, was a picture of a guy in gym class. He was shinnying a rope. I couldn't get my own gym classes out of my mind. I wanted the guy to make it to the top of the rope and to get an A, but he wouldn't cooperate. The bastard kept falling to the floor until he hurt his damn back and had to go to the nurse. I thought it was a piss-poor story, but the shrink loved it. She called it significant. I thought she was a loser just like the guy on the rope.

Then I filled out questionnaires. It was back to school with these true false questions and a number two pencil. Yeah, I said, my table manners are as good in private as they are in public. Hell, I wouldn't lie about something like that. My table manners suck everywhere.

The whole thing was a pain in my ass, but eventually they stopped studying me like bug crap, and then I got to talk, to really talk.

I talked about the terror I felt as a kid. I talked a lot about Stan. He was my cousin – my cousin and my closest friend. Then he pulled his motorcycle out of this scenic rest stop in California; he pulled out right in front of a concrete truck. They scraped him off the pavement and cremated what was left. Since he'd done the same thing in the same place a year earlier but had survived that time, I figured he was trying. If at first you don't succeed, try, try again. If you still don't succeed, give up; don't make a damn fool of yourself. Stan hadn't made a damn fool of himself, just a blot. Ink blots and blood blots, what's the difference?

Stan was two years older than I, which made him my source of knowledge in the world of childhood. The trouble was that Stan saw the world through horror colored glasses. He passed his understanding of the world's woes onto me – at least until he found his messy way of escaping them.

His ashes were sprinkled around his college campus, the place he had been least unhappy. I have no idea if the wind was blowing that day, but I hope some ash ended tearing an eye. Everybody deserves a few tears.

***

Was Stan the reason I live in fear?

Who the hell knows?

Maybe we both inherited the damn fear gene.

Maybe we both had to live with screaming angry fathers who intimidated us as often as they could. With my old man nothing was ever good enough. My uncle was another story. He just raged. It didn't matter what Stan or his sister did. It didn't matter what Aunt Alice did. Uncle John just raged.

Then, when he had gotten it all out, he'd retreat into his study. He'd stay locked in there for days. He had a connecting bathroom, a sofa to sleep on, his easel, on which he could paint and repaint the same awful picture of a clipper ship being tossed onto the rocks by the grayness of tormented seas and tortured skies; and he had the meals that his wife, my aunt, dutifully left on trays by the door.

The days would pass. His store would go unopened; his customers would go unserved. Then, without warning, he'd reappear, act normally for a few days, slowly descend into another cloud of rage, and repeat the cycle of his special madness.

Some of us land in the morgue, some of us land in the asylum, and some of us build our own asylums. It's all the same. It is, in the end, all the same.

CHAPTER TWO

"Sometimes you feel like a nut, sometimes you don't." The voice echoing down the yellow-green corridors sounds like bagpipes.

Yes, that was it, bagpipes. Marilyn remembers the pipers marching around the little square of her hometown – or was it really hers?

She had been surprised by their kilts. Weren't kilts supposed to be red? The pipers wore a tartan of multiple grays. Her father held her hand, and her mother held her brother's. It had been a wonderful holiday.

Her little brother jumped up and down with excitement. "Look at their knives," he shouted, pointing simultaneously to the dirks tucked at their waists and the ones tucked into their right leggings. "I'll bet they could slit your throat with one swipe." He had been so excited, running in circles and pointing in every direction.

"I'd run away," she responded. It had been a simple declaration of safety. Marilyn was the quiet child; her brother provided enough uproar for them both. "I'd run away and hide." The thought of hiding had pleased her.

The crack in the plaster opposite her bed opens up. She doesn't want it to. She never does. It is the doorway into the place of memories of the future and forgets of the past. It is hers and hers alone. It is her torment and her pain; it is her pleasure and her safety.

Beyond it lies a forest. She has been in the forest many times. As a girl, she recalls, she had sat beneath the beech tree and watched the skunks playing. She had liked them, and they had liked her. Rosie they hadn't liked. He had come home, his eyes stung and smelling awfully of their fear. That was what came of being a fox terrier. Fox terriers didn't know how to sit quietly. They didn't know how to run away. They only knew how to bounce up and down, how to run in circles, how to make barking sounds – how to be like her brother.

The sounds had not meant much to her as a child. Not the sounds of the forest, and even less the sounds of other people. Sometimes there was music. That she understood; that had been the sound of meaning. There has always been music, and sometimes it is here with her within the wall, within the crack in the plaster across from her bed.

The brass band, dressed in yellow uniforms, is playing Sousa marches in the gazebo. Not many towns have a gazebo anymore. It was a shame that they cut streets through the park. They cut streets, and they cut down the trees that were still there. Of course, the elms had already died;

they had dropped their Dutched branches and been cut for burial. That was how things went, and went, and went away.

But at least they left the gazebo and a few benches so the old men could come and listen to the Sousa marches and talk about great wars and poison gases, about depressions and victories, about how things had been and what they would become. She liked the man with the shrapnel-pocked legs who gave her candy even though her mother told him not to. He said that he had run away from the gas, but he hadn't run fast enough because the shrapnel got him anyway. Marilyn wondered if she could have run away fast enough. "Marilyn be nimble, Marilyn be quick, Marilyn avoid the shrapnel and the death."

The man said that lots of horses had died in the battles. Marilyn wondered about the songs of dying horses. Sometimes she tried to sing the songs for them, but her voice drowned out the melody.

There were songs to be sung, bells to be rung.

Once she had tried to ring out a bell to take all the sound out of it until no one could hear it except God.

It had been the bell that held the bats. She hated bats.

In the summer when they went to the lake, there would be bats in the chimney. Her father would lay a fire, and she could hear the bats shriek as they slowly roasted and fell into the embers. It was a ritual. Her father would make stern harrumphs, her mother would tsk-tsk, her brother would screech his excitement, and Marilyn would cover her ears and be a silent witness, a witness to the gruesomeness, a witness to the terror – a witness to herself.

Johnny had once told her that Jews would slaughter Christians to make matzo. She wondered if that was why her father roasted the bats. Maybe they were Christian bats. They sometimes played softball in school, but she hated to bat. When the ball came at her she wanted to run. Running away was a good thing to do. Staying safe. The world through the crack in the yellow-green plaster opposite her bed, that was safe, too.

***

"Almond Joy has nuts, Mounds don't." The bagpipes are coming closer. Marilyn knows about bagpipes, how they led the troops into glorious battle. Glorious battle: was there such a thing? How did you die in glory? She has never seen glory. But she has seen death.

Death had been slow and painful. Cancer had taken over her mother from the inside out. They said it had grown in her, but to Marilyn it was more as if the cancer had eaten her, making her smaller and smaller until only the squeak of death remained – a painful squeak, a high-pitched bat squeak of agony.

Inside the crack she can see her mother's body. Her X-ray vision pierces the outer layers, and she can see the giant cancer eating the remaining entrails. It is a worm, a massive worm, with a thousand heads. On each head is a mouth with hundreds of sharp teeth – razor teeth. She hears her mother screaming in agony. Marilyn wills herself to get up – to run towards her and help, to run away towards safety. Her body remains locked in itself.

She lies in the thin-blanketed bed. She lies propped on the rough cotton pillows. She is as she has been propped. Marilyn moves not. Only her memory moves – her memory and her terror.

The nurse with the black hair and the bloodshot eyes had propped Marilyn up that morning. She had coaxed a few spoons of oatmeal or Cream of Wheat or whatever down her throat. Marilyn likes to watch the black haired nurse with the bloodshot eyes feed her; she is so dexterous with the napkin. The drools and dribbles are wiped away before they can stain her bedclothes.

Marilyn has always appreciated people who are good at their work. She tries to be good at her work, too. What if her work is to do nothing, what if it is to lie immobile and watch the world of mysteries that unfolds within the wall opposing, what if it is to drool and dribble: she still wants to do it well.

It isn't easy being a schizophrenic. It takes effort to stay hidden. If she makes a mistake, even a little one, she will be found out. "See how careful the mouse is to stay still. He hopes the cat won't see him hiding there. But if she sees him, he'll jump back inside the hole where she can't follow him."

But the cat did catch the mouse. She had seen her eating him. Throwing him up and down in the air like a little ball until, tired with her game, she snapped his body apart. *The mouse should never have come out of his hole*, Marilyn thinks. *He should have stayed in there except when it was rainy, or snowy, or cloudy, or night, or not sunny anyway. That is the best thing of all. It always is.* She wonders if she could make a sign warning cats to stay away. Can cats read? That is a question worth pondering.

If cats could read, they wouldn't like the books in first grade. There are too many dogs in the first grade, far too many dogs. All the dogs are named Spot.

She told the teacher that her dog's name was Rosie, and the teacher told her that was okay. She didn't mean to ask the teacher's permission for her dog to be Rosie. His name was Rosie because that was what his grandmother had named him. That must have been so because she had been named for her grandmother who had died before Marilyn was born.

Her grandfather hadn't died. He couldn't have. He couldn't have died, because nobody knew who he was. If he didn't have a name, how could he stop being whoever it was he was?

Sometimes it's just safer to not be who you are supposed to be. She wonders if she might stop being Marilyn, or if she could be somebody else for a change. Somebody else might live behind the crack that is in the wall of the room, the wall opposite her bed.

No, she must still be Marilyn because she lives in that crack, the one opposite her pillow, the one with the dead elms, and the beech tree and the bagpipes, and the skunks, and the shrieking bats, and the deadly knives, and the cancer-worm eating her mother. That is who she is; that is who she must be.

It isn't easy knowing who one is. It takes a lot of time for her to rehearse and remind herself. Some days she forgets. Those are bad days, days when she is too frightened to hide. Then she grabs hold of everything she can before she is drowned in the nothingness. She grabs the nurses and the attendants.

Sometimes Celia, who sings about candy bars, comes in to see her screaming and listen to her writhing, and Marilyn grabs her, too. Then they give her a shot in the butt, and she goes to sleep.

When she wakes, she is always less frightened but more terrified. It is as if she were drowning and has tried to grab hold of some passing piece of wood. Trying to grab the wood is terrifying. When she awakes, the wood will be gone along with the terror, but she feels all that much more lost at sea.

She almost drowned once. Her father had rented a motorboat, and they had gone out on a huge lake. The motor died, and the wind came up. Her father, standing in the boat and trying to restart the motor, had capsized them. They clung to the overturned rowboat until the man who rented it to them came looking. Twice she slipped off the bottom of the boat and gone under the water. Both times her mother grabbed her and dragged her back to the air. But she knew that if she had gone under a third time that would have been that.

Marilyn knows that life is scary. It is too easy to go down for a third time.

She wonders if the cancer-worm had already been eating her mother from the inside out when they had been clinging to the boat.

Would it find her here, hiding?

Her father had found her. When his wife died and he had gone unsatisfied, he had found her with his worm. In the dark of the night, hiding in the black, she had been found and cut.

The keen of the bagpipes joins the scream of protest that rises in her throat only to die in her ears and in the crack – the crack that is all truth.

CHAPTER THREE

"That's gross!"

"You think so?"

"I know so. It's… It's God-damned disgusting."

"I suppose."

"You suppose? I know! How the hell could he do that?"

"I don't know. I guess it was some kind of compulsion, something beyond his control."

"You don't believe that, do you?"

"Yeah. I guess I do."

"Look, there are limits."

"I'm not excusing him. I can't excuse him. I doubt he can excuse himself."

"Nobody could." He pauses. "How the hell did he find somebody that young? You'd think the mother would have been watching."

"It was his daughter."

"Christ, his own kid?"

"Uh-huh."

"That's grosser than gross. It totally barfs me out."

"I suppose."

"There you go with your supposes again. I mean, how disgusting is it? To fuck your own baby."

"Yeah!"

"And kill her."

"Yeah."

"And then cook her up and eat her for dinner. Jesus!"

"Yeah, but he had to be crazy."

"Crazy? We're crazy. We don't do things like that. They ought to fry his ass, not put him in here."

"It certainly could give us a bad reputation."

"As opposed to our present good one?"

"You know what I mean."

"I was just kidding."

"Shit, this isn't something to kid about."

Arthur and I are pacing up and down the dayroom. That way the aides don't notice. As long as we look agitated, they don't care about our conversations. They figure we must be ourselves: the simply crazy. If we were to sit down on the bilious green Naugahyde and chrome chairs and couches that have long since deteriorated to junkyard quality and talk like normal people, then they'd get pissed off. They count on us to be psycho, to appear nuts. It's like the cops and the criminals. The criminals might not want the cops around, but the cops need the crooks so they have jobs. And, if the cops disappeared then everyone could commit the same criminal acts so there'd be no payoff for being a crook. So, bottom line, the staff needs us to keep getting their paychecks, and we need them to keep getting our rubber-rooms, straightjackets, and butts full of Valium.

But, the numbers are changing. The psycho drugs have reduced the size of all the hospitals. The staffs have shrunk; now they're resisting every discharge. No normality here! Nobody should get out. That's the rule.

So we are pacing and discussing the alleged newest member of our very nonselective club. Of course, it is all rumor and conjecture. The rolling TV never plays the news; it's considered too upsetting.

Newspapers and magazines only make an appearance when an infrequent visitor happens to bring them, which is always well after they're better suited for wrapping fish. Visitors are few and far between. We who have survived the medication boom and still live on the wards have few family members interested in us. The aides and nurses do bring gossipy magazines that they share with each other and then leave around for us. We always know the latest tittle-tattle from three weeks ago. We can always tell that our bleached out castaway clothing isn't the latest from Paris.

"Maybe. But, then what's to stop them from frying every nut case," I pause for effect, "including us?"

"Would you do something like that?"

"No."

"Well, neither would I."

"Of course not, but you did attack those people."

He giggles nervously. "God told me to."

"I know, but maybe God told him."

He raises his voice, always a foolish thing to do, but theology is always a hot button in the day room. "God would never tell him that – not something like that!"

One of the aides looks up at us. I catch her out of the corner of my eye, the one that I always keep directed at the nurses' station.

"Sshhh," I hiss at him. But he is way too far-gone. God's prophet is on the pulpit, and nothing else matters. It only takes a minute before they drug him, wrap him, and carry him off to restraints.

They might decide I should get it, too, that I have been provoking him, that I might get others started – that I might be the "King of the Crazies" – and they talk about our paranoia. I walk away as fast as I can.

Too late! They have grabbed me and wrestled my ass to the floor. I'm not resisting. There would be no point. They still rough me up. One aide, this big hulk of an idiot, a sadist too afraid to take on anyone who can fight back, smacks me in the face – no reason, just his pleasure. My nose starts to bleed. They hold me down so that I'm coughing and choking on my own damn blood. One of the nurses brings the syringe. The big V to the rescue.

I wake up the next day on the medical ward. There is a hole in my throat where they inserted a tracheotomy tube. The bastard has nearly killed me. God, is my throat sore. I get to suck on ice chips and suffer. The bastard got to go home for his dinner.

A day later I am back on the ward. One of the women patients sidles over to me. "We heard they had to give you shock treatments," she hisses.

"No," I croak back pointing at my throat.

"I thought your brains were up here," she says pointing to her head.

I try to laugh and then think better of it. I pat my ass. "No, down here," I tell her.

She is still cackling as one of the nurses came out from behind their counter with the medication tray. My pills are different. I look at them and then at her. "Take your meds," she commands firmly.

"They aren't right."

"The doctor changed them."

"Why?"

"Ask him."

"Come on, at least tell me why," I plead, afraid of the side effects.

"We want to make sure that you behave yourself. No more incidents like yesterday.

I want to cry, but I just nod. I try to hold some of the pills in my cheek to spit them out once she has gone, but she checks my mouth and makes me take a second cup of the horrible juice they use. It tastes like a combination of the bug-juice they serve at summer camp and some powdered fruit drink straight from the army, and filled with saltpeter.

"Be a good boy," she says as she walks away. I feel like I'm a dog being patted absentmindedly on the head by a totally indifferent and unfeeling clerk in a department store. "You really shouldn't have your dog in here, mister; but keep him under control and we won't shoot you full of meds."

"Yes, ma'am; yes, ma'am, three bags full."

No matter how fucked your head, you've got to hate the drooling and the shuffling. I try to control the tics and that damned unending pill rolling. I try, but I fail – failure is in the chemistry.

I know that eventually they'll cut back. They always do because the now-patientized patient won't have gotten in any trouble, and somebody counts the pills or at least the cost of the pills and says "too many". Then they'll cut back; and the tics will disappear, my thumbs and forefingers will stop their strange exercise in mid-brain limbo, and the drool will stop playing me for a basset hound.

Hell, I won't be getting into trouble. I can't get into trouble; I can barely move. I sit and I stare, mostly at that damn rolling TV screen, sometimes at space, other times at the imaginary TV screen rolling in space. Thoughts come slow and hard; they're disconnected from emotions. I'm floating in a mindless sea of mud – mind mud, shit brown and sucking. Slowly, I'm descending into a primeval tar pit. I'm becoming extinct; I'm slowly joining the dinosaurs – a lumbering beast has taken over my soul.

I know that eventually they'll cut back.

The pedophilic-infantaciding-cannibal never comes to our ward. It doesn't matter. He has taken his small chunk out of my brain.

CHAPTER FOUR

"I won't do it."

"I don't think we get a choice on this."

"She should be in a nursing home."

"There's nothing wrong with her."

"What the hell does that mean? She just lies there like a vegetable."

"I meant nothing physical."

"She's still a vegetable."

"She eats."

"If you feed her."

"She sees."

"How do you know?"

"Because her eyes follow you around the room."

"But what is she seeing?"

"That's something you could ask about most of these crazies."

This new aide is pissed – really, really pissed. A burly guy, John, who looks more like he should be working in a steel mill or chopping down trees, but there are no mills, mines, or forests, not around here. We're the industry, the factory: human waste management at its most medical.

John is following petite Carol with the big fake boobs, the shift supervisor, around the ward. "I still don't understand why I have to change her diapers," he whines.

"Because it's one of our jobs – correction, one of your jobs. You said that you've changed diapers before, didn't you?"

"My kids, once or twice. I'm not no baby sitter."

"Well, that's exactly what you are now, only some of these babies can get pretty damn violent."

"Her?" he asks with a snort, gesturing back toward Marilyn's room.

"Not at the moment. Who knows?" she replies resignedly. Carol doesn't look very happy this morning. It has gotten off to one bad start. Mitch managed to throw one of the Naugahyde chairs and hit Sue, who, bleeding profusely, had to go to the medical unit. That meant that there was one aide off the ward – one less pair of hands, one less set of muscles. With this new John, who doesn't know what to do or want to do it, and with Mitch bouncing off the walls, Carole actually had to get physically involved. In the process of subduing Mitch she had managed to get herself kicked in the boobs.

That had to hurt. Was she going to spill silicone blood? Who knew? Personally, I figure breaking a falsie is like telling the truth – something good to do until you get caught, then all hell breaks out.

Now, Carol's day is getting worse. This new John guy is already making the kinds of sounds that don't bode well. She knows that if the local job market were any better, he'd be gone. Hell, if there were a local job market, he'd be gone. That might have been better for all of us, but who knows what piece of shit would replace this piece of shit. On the other hand, what doesn't come out today just gives you a pain till it gets crapped out tomorrow. Any way you looked at it, our lives were in the toilet. We're in the toilet and that water is circling faster and faster – right near the bottom and just about to flush out.

From time to time the aides have been talking about some foreign company building a cabinet and door plant in town. Of course, we've heard that story a lot of times. The town is always trying to attract some new businesses. It seems the deals always fall through. I wonder if maybe the managers and CEOs might not object to being around all us nutcases. Maybe they figure schizophrenia is catchy. Who knows, maybe it is.

If they built that plant or some other plant, this new guy, John, would be one of the first to go. That much is clear. In the meantime, I make a note to stay clear of him. He's the kind that can do you real harm. He's big, he's strong, and he doesn't give a damn. He's replacing the guy who caused my tracheotomy. No, that guy wasn't fired. The powers that be decided he was the kind of powerhouse they needed on the maximum-security ward. When I heard they had moved him, I wondered if it was a promotion or a punishment. Then I figured it out. It wasn't either; it was just one of those pragmatic moves – tough guy for a tough crowd. At least they weren't giving him a bounty.

I had been told once – in another life – that at some automobile dealerships the mechanics would give money to help suckers buy certain models, the ones with unending high-priced repairs. I wondered if the people who worked the medical ward did the same thing with the aides. "Mess a few guys up because our business is slow and we'll take care of you." Isn't that how the world works? No wonder I'm so damn scared of it. Now, if you're rich, most of the time you don't have to be nuts to play safe; you just pay the world off. And they say money doesn't buy happiness. Hell, in here, I can buy lots of it with a pack of smokes.

As low man on the totem pole, the new aide has gotten the shit details. Often they are real shit details – and piss, puke and blood. Change Marilyn's diapers; clean the smeared feces off the walls; clean up the blood from the patient who was hurt; mop up the piss when somebody starts marking territory. Great job! For this he gets a whopping ten bucks an hour. But his family survives. Of course, they could all check in here and get room and board courtesy of the state. The board isn't too good. Most of the beds aren't in private rooms, and your back aches in the morning. The bathrooms stink – in fact, the whole place stinks. And the help is nasty. But what the hell, it's home.

Anyway, he does it – sort of. He changes her diapers. Marilyn doesn't make a sound. By the next shift she has diaper rash. I wonder if, when he had taken care of his kids, he had just slapped another diaper on and waited for mom to come home from her shift at Wal-Mart to do the ass cleaning.

Some of us wonder if they were to let Marilyn's rash get worse, would she react and show some intelligent life, or would she go into one of those unintelligible fits of screaming and grabbing. It is one of those little details that can provide you with endless discussions in a world of so little information.

The next day, Carol takes John aside and asks if he really wants to be an aide. She thinks that they are having a private conversation. They aren't.

In mental hospitals, the staff forget that the patients have ears. In fact, they tend to think of the patients as pieces of furniture that occasionally move around – like the chair that Mitch threw yesterday – inanimate objects subject to inexplicable forces.

"I have to work," John answers with surprising honesty. "I've got a family to feed, and we need the medical coverage."

"Fine, then adjust your attitude. If you let something slide, somebody else ends up with more work. Then people complain. I don't want to hear it. Worse, if they start complaining up the food chain, then I'm in trouble. I don't like trouble. I don't like listening to some dumb ration of shit. You don't have to like the loonies; just do your job."

"Yeah, sure." I can see on his face that Marilyn – poor, helpless Marilyn lying in her catatonic stupor – will pay the price for getting that rash.

Harry has been listening, too. "How long before he quits?"

"Too long," I answer, "especially for Marilyn."

I go to Marilyn's room to check on her. I figure I'd better do it before I forget. I know it won't keep the pain away, but it's my little atonement for… for what?… for not being able to protect her… or myself.

She lays there as she always does. "Life sucks," I say to her. I know she won't answer. Hell, I'm not even sure she can hear me. What does that matter? It's true. Life sucks. It sucks and then you die. There's no way to be sure, but I figure that dying sucks even more. That's one big difference between me and some of the others here, the ones who keep trying to off themselves, people like my cousin.

Stan kept fish, tropical fish, and liked jazz. He played jazz records for the fish and tried to give them safe places to breed. He was caring, and he was bright - bright enough for the Ivy League. He became an engineer. Bad choice. He wasn't the engineering type, too introspective, too concerned with ideas and values. Back then engineering was a guaranteed job – at least that was what people thought. It was before the day of brilliant Indians shipped from Bangalore with work visas. It was before computers, too, at least the ones that sit on your desk or even your lap. The computers that did exist were monsters that devoured punch cards and needed huge air-conditioned rooms. Back then engineers still used slide rules and pencils.

Now engineers are interchangeable. Maybe they were then, too, but people didn't think about it. People thought about jobs, careers, stay at one company and retire with a pension and benefits. Boy, were they fooled. Stan didn't stay around long enough to be fooled. He rode his motorcycle into the path of that truck and avoided the years of disappointment that we call life.

Nobody wanted to admit it was suicide. They insisted it had been a tragic accident. I guess that made it easier for them. Either way, he was dead. All things considered, Stan should have run a fish store or sold records and stayed happy. All things considered, it probably didn't matter then and matters less now. On the cosmic scale, does God really care if somebody becomes an engineer or not, if they run a fish store or not, if they're locked in the asylum or not? Does God really care? If He does, I'd like to know why. But then, there are lots of whys that I'd like to know.

CHAPTER FIVE

"Dr. Abrose!" There is a pause. "Dr. Abrose!!" His voice is getting slightly louder and more demanding. It disturbs me; it rouses me from the fantasy of my moment. It is a recurring fantasy, the one in which my father admits that he has been wrong. It is a fantasy that warms me – mental comfort food, tapioca for the mind of the fear ridden.

"Yes, sir."

"Are you following me?"

"I think so, sir. It's just that there seems to be so much."

"This is an efficiently run institution. You'll get the best training in the world here, but you have to pull your share." The speaker's gray hair is neatly combed back, leaving a wide forehead between his hairline and the horned rimmed glasses with the thick glass, which perch on the end of his nose.

Looking at the administrative director of the hospital, Dr. Buford Abrose, first year resident, is aware of a churning in his stomach. *The man has no eyes*, he realizes. It isn't that Dr. Partles is blind, although, given the thickness of his glasses, he might be close to it. It is that Dr. Abrose feels like there are no eyes – no eyes at all – behind those thick glasses. If eyes are the windows of the soul, then Orrin Partles's soul is surely unavailable to inspection.

Buford Abrose is one of the three new residents who will be starting at the asylum this month. He is, it happens, the first to arrive. Therefore, he is getting his very own individualized tour. He had been delighted at the opportunity to get to know his supervising administrator, but now he isn't so sure. After a perfunctory handshake, Partles has led him quickly through the units, all the while explaining the importance of various forms and reports. There had not been a single mention of a specific patient, only sweeping descriptions of units: "This unit is the schizophrenic women who are slated for discharge."

"Here we have the depressed geriatrics."

Dr. Abrose wonders if the older man might not have been happier running a department store. "Manic depressives? Yes, ma'am, third floor just to the right of the escalators." "Obsessive-compulsives? Only available on third Mondays after full-moons." "Anxiety disorders: hiding under aisle seven."

"The Medicaid forms, they're due on Mondays at eleven. That's important. They have to be out in the Tuesday mail, or we lose a week on the payment."

Buford Abrose's internship had been unrewarding. He had delivered more babies than he had seen people in need of psychiatric care, although, given their inner -city financial situations, he wondered about the sanity of most of those new mothers. He did not enjoy delivering new life. Singularly insensitive to those mothers and their coming newborns, he performed most of the deliveries half riding on the gurneys making their way from waiting area to delivery room. Luckily the women, too poor to complain and too used to getting by to make extra work of the births, had little need of his assistance. They dropped their children and went on living while he, the would-be doctor, read Freud, Sullivan, and Kohut, and obsessed about his childhood and dreams.

That internship had been at a general community hospital in a Midwestern rust-haven city. Buford often wondered what possessed him to choose it and then would remember Helen's advice. He had always looked up to her, a successful attending with a good family practice who seemed so caring while he desperately burrowed his way to the end of medical school. She was the friendliest woman he had ever met. Everybody described her as "well-meaning;" the fourth year students often turned to her for guidance. He wondered how many of them had over the years been given equally poor advice.

She, knowing that he wanted to be a psychiatrist, had deliberately recommended a hospital where psychiatry was limited to occasionally detoxing a drunk or sedating someone waiting for transportation to a state hospital.

It was only after he had been at Dunford Community for a month that Buford realized how deliberate she had been. Helen felt he belonged in family practice – she felt that way about all young doctors, and that had been her way of making him realize what was best for him. The road to purgatory is lined with the good wishes of the well meaning. Now he would pay the additional price of doing his residency in this God-forsaken state hospital at which his colleagues would be graduates of fifth rate medial schools from Caribbean islands and doctors from India who were waiting to take their English competency exams. He swore to himself that he would find an analytic program to enter – a good dose of Freud to counteract psychiatry by restraint.

"Dr. Abrose!" Dr. Partles is getting irritated with Buford's frequent lapses of attention.

"I understood, sir. By restricting access to the medications it forces the doctors to write clearer orders. But what about emergency situations?"

"There are no emergencies here. Good orderly administration gives good orderly ward life. Don't you agree?"

"Well, sir, I'm hardly experienced enough to have an opinion." Buford is beginning to hate himself for the ass-kissing way he is talking. He hasn't even called the older man Doctor, let alone by name. It reminded him of boarding school. He had spent the first month at Chumsfield wondering if they still caned kids. He had read and seen the movie version of "Tom Brown's School Days" and expected to find Chumsfield very much the same.

***

Chumsfield had been another mistake, the first of that long line. It had been his and his alone. His parents had passively allowed Buford to choose which boarding school he would attend. That he would go to boarding school had been decided for him. His father's deepening depression, his mother's black-cloud of helpless loneliness, the day-to-day degeneration of his family: these were put into inevitable motion on one fateful suicided day. Chumsfield, or some place like it, was the unavoidable result of that chaotic family motion combined with money from an insurance company willing to settle rather than face what would certainly have been a hostile jury.

So, feeling rejected by his family, Buford had chosen deliberately, if unwisely. Chumsfield was old, English-styled, aristocratic, formal, high-church, and everything else that the Abrose family no longer was. If Buford had been more self-aware, if he had been better able to put into words, he might have said, "If you'll not have me, then I'll reject you as well." But he had not been able, and he did not say. He simply went off to a world that sneered at him from the moment of his arrival until his eventual lonely leaving.

The school's neatly cared grounds and venerable buildings were at odds with Buford's working class city worldview. Accents and sports jackets, neckties and generations of connections: everything marked him an outsider. Even if his family had bothered with Brooks Brothers and the Harvard Shop, with gray flannel, with lacrosse and real bowties, he would have stood out. As it was, he became a laughingstock. The studying and the eventual good grades only made Buford stand even more apart.

At Chumsfield sports were more important than scholarship. The trophies in the lobby of Duncan Gymnasium, the team pictures placed row on row to record the pride of the academy, the announcements of victories past and yet to come at meals and worship made the school's priorities clear. If sports were regnant, they were always juxtaposed to heroism on the field of battle. Prayers and hymns were regularly offered for the souls of alumni who had died in wars. The first had been The War Between the States, a war in which Chumsfield alumni served with heroic distinction on both sides.

Buford was not the stuff of heroes, athletic or other. He managed the soccer team, played intramural basketball, and played at golf in the spring. Boarding school heroes were made of more physical stuff. There was no one at Chumsfield who cared that he read Tolstoy or Freud or Kant. They cared that he wasn't tough enough to play sports or interested in the rough and tumble of adolescent boys trying to displace their sexual energies when deprived of girls.

He had on a few occasions slipped out of the dorm and joined up with Pete and Jack, his best friends, or, more correctly, his best acquaintances. Pete was a day student and looked down on by the other boarders. Jack Brogden was the son of one of the masters, an English teacher who coached no sport, talked about Shakespeare, and commanded no respect. Jack loved his father, and therefore disliked the students who held him in contempt. Even though he was athletic enough to perhaps earn their acceptance, Jack preferred to hang out with Buford and Pete and any other boys who didn't fit in.

Once the three boys had built a fire in the woods and gotten drunk on whiskey they had stolen from Mr. Nash, the Latin master who was better at declining brands of gin than adjectives.

It did occur to Buford that Mr. Nash might miss the bottles, but the teacher emptied too many himself to be able to keep track of the number carefully lined along the railing of the porch outside his residence. The boys always wondered how Mrs. Nash could put up with the drinking until they realized that she was often at Mr. Donovan's rooms while her husband was doing his thing on the playing fields of Chumsfield – on the playing fields where character was made.

By then Buford had also realized how absurd the entire boarding school experience was, but during that first month he had been scared and overwhelmed. His answer then had been to be obsequious, just as he was doing now as he followed Dr. Partles from form to form and from regulation to locked door.

CHAPTER SIX

Doris is excited – very excited. She's always excited when a new doctor is assigned to our ward. That excitement is intensified if the doctor is male. If he's good looking, then she becomes ecstatic. This new resident with his quick smile and his full head of close-cropped brown hair more than meets her requirements. Ecstasy is hers.

Doris is a hair fanatic. Her own is dyed a gaudy, unnatural shade of red that somehow goes with her moonscape-creased face and her dry cracked skin. Her lipstick, which she applies and reapplies with a heavy hand and without benefit of a looking glass, is equally bright and garish. Overly rouged and mascara-ed and smelling of cheap perfume named, no doubt, Irresistible, Doris gives the impression of an elderly hooker desperately hanging on – clinging to her spot on the worst corner in town. She is a caricature of sex, a cartoon of magazine-fueled femininity, and absolutely, totally, completely terrified of any sexual actuality.

Even the sickest aides, the ones who work the night shift and come creeping into our beds in the middle of the night like necrophiliac vampires, avoid Doris for fear that she might return to the frenzied dementia of her first appearance on the ward. She had, it is said, been a bookkeeper; one of those people who live orderly, measured lives, following routines that turn existence into ciphers and leave no marks that can't easily be rubbed away. Then, one spring afternoon, while walking home from the market – ironically a Safeway market – she was dragged into a doorway, brutally raped, and left in a dehumanized rag-dressed heap for the sanitation department to remove.

This one sexual experience of her life would have been more than she could have borne, but it was followed by the worst of psychological consequences: pregnancy. Her religious beliefs forbade abortion, so she had carried the child, a little boy, who – perhaps with God's mercy – had died within hours of birth. His death had been the last cruel blow of this furious assault on her being, the one that had produced Doris – our Doris – the terrified flirt of the ward: a whore who lives in terror of sex, a cartoon at which even the mad cannot laugh.

While many of us would put on a show for any new doctor to make sure we got the attention that we so richly didn't deserve, no one else could ever come near to Doris's personal extravaganza, the one she is performing for Buford Abrose, M.D, the new resident. It is truly a work of beauty. Waiting until her target is facing in her direction and at least half the dayroom away from her, she does a shimmying cakewalk toward him, half stripping as she undulates across the room. On reaching him, she wraps her arms and legs around him in a dry hump, pulls him towards her, and, sticking her tongue into his mouth, kisses him square on the lips, leaving the imprint of her thick, bright magenta lipstick, making him at once her fellow clown and a little boy guilty for having drunk all the strawberry milk.

Buford pulls back from Doris's embrace with a suitable expression of horror and embarrassment. Carol goes with swift determination to the nurses' station and comes back with a handful of tissues. She hands them to the doctor and says, "Now you've been properly welcomed to the ward."

The young doctor stands paralyzed by this sudden violation of madness. He stares, uncomprehendingly, at his libidinous attacker. His Freudian texts have not prepared him for this, not for authentic patient contact nor for the full-flowered brilliance of schizophrenia.

I could have told him - could have warned him. The books are about language, about people talking. Schizophrenia is more real. "What can be shown cannot be said." A philosopher said that, but we crazies live it. Words are just actions; actions are communications; everything is illusion; hallucinations are the currency of life, the current that flows through the livewires of us.

I could have told him – could have warned him. But that would have required a change of identity, from self-absorbed madness to normal social concern. It would have required my admission of knowledge, of thought, of awareness. That would have blown my cover. We are all in our ways secret agents; the cover of the mad is greater than most. It allows us to know without admission and to be aware without responsibility.

I could have told him – could have warned him. The drums had spoken, the rumors had flown. We had known more about him before his arrival than he would ever know about us. Oh, he would have the folder, those notes created by unawareness and insensitivity. He would have interpretations of inkblots and such. He would have histories given by self-protective relatives. He would have the data of misinformation, but we would have the truth of grapevines and the wisdom of survival.

While Buford Abrose is wiping the garish from his face, one of the other aides has already taken Doris firmly by the arm and is leading her, unprotesting, to one of those horribly chrome chairs. Firmly, pushing her down, the aide commands loudly enough for all to hear and heed, "Don't go bothering the doctor or you'll find yourself getting a needle."

The rest of us, as if commanded by some dance caller, become immediately stirred and roiled. The threat is genuine, but the determination to be noticed is also real. There is a fractional momentary silence, a brief hesitancy. Then Mitch does what Mitch does best: he throws things.

Almost at once, the entire ward is in a bedlam of revolution. Even Charlie, poor shuffling, brain-gone Charlie, is howling like a wolf baying at a witches' moon. Mixed with his howls are echolalic shouts of "Oh, boy! Oh, boy!" Only Doris and Marilyn are quiet. Doris sits in her chair like a princess on a throne. She surveys her realm with the satisfaction of the truly crazed, of the politician at war, of the miser collecting rent, of the coward being led from battle.

And Marilyn, poor, catatonic Marilyn, sits strapped in her geri-chair as she does on any day that the staff has bothered to take her from her bed. Because John is on duty and it is his lowly responsibility, nobody has wheeled the chair into the dayroom. Instead, she sits inert in her room. She stares at the crack in the wall opposite her bed. She stares at nothing, and she sees the world.

CHAPTER SEVEN

It is another bumperpool day. Marilyn can always tell. They are propping her on the edge of the bed and sliding her feet into the fuzzy pink slippers that have somehow found their way into her life and become a part of who she is. It is always that way in the asylum; the inmate owns nothing yet certain things become uniquely hers.

Holding her up, they are pushing Marilyn's unwilling arms into the white bathrobe which then hangs untied on her skinny, sagging frame as if she is a wire coat hanger. Then they wheel the chair next to her and let her drop into it. It is a tall wooden straight-backed chair with small wheels on the back legs, wheels like the ones on grocery carts. Next comes the tray; it slides into place holding her chest and locking so that she cannot push free. Her legs are bound with leather straps to end any possibility of self-propulsion. Yet, if Marilyn were to propel herself with intent to anywhere at any time, it would be considered a therapeutic miracle.

No, firmly chaired, she is tipped back and wheeled, inert baggage, into the dayroom. There she and her chair are pushed against a death-yellow wall. There she is left. She is to remain until someone should decide to rearrange – to rearrange the objects, the furniture, the things.

She is going nowhere while other people in drooping white robes and stained pajamas or ill-fitting God-knows-how-many-times hand-me down clothes walk back and forth also go nowhere. Their yellow stained fingers hold an unending supply of cigarettes smoked to the edge of those shaking fingers; the ashes drop and scatter on smokers, furniture, floor, and on her. It doesn't matter – ashes to ashes, dust to nothing.

***

As a child Marilyn had, oh-so enjoyed playing bumperpool. Timmy Wang, whose father, Wang Po, owned the local variety store, would invite her to play. First, they would play with the toys tossed into the glass-separated bins along the aisles of the store. Then they would go in back, where Timmy and his father lived, and they would play bumperpool.

Marilyn had never been very good at games, but she felt a special affinity for bumperpool. The idea that no matter where she wanted to go she somehow would be blocked seemed to make sense to her.

It was good that some things made sense, because so many didn't. She didn't understand why Mrs. Gilroy didn't think that Mr. Wang should run the variety store. "He should have a laundry or a restaurant." As usual, Marilyn was listening from the next room and trying to make sense of the grown-up world. Her father said that Mrs. Gilroy had an uninformed opinion about everything. Marilyn didn't understand that, either.

Timmy Wang liked to poke at Marilyn. He liked to make believe that he was a bumperpool cue and that she was a ball. When they were young he just poked her anywhere. When she got older, he poked her in the breasts. His fingers – then even more yellowed by the cigarettes he enlessly smoked – had gentled with time but had also grown insistent. Marilyn didn't understand why Timmy liked to poke her. She didn't understand why Timmy liked to poke her breasts, but she didn't object. Timmy was her friend, and bumperpool was their bond.

One day Timmy changed the game. He took his pants down and pulled hers down, too. She looked down at his small, hairless penis. "What's that?" she asked.

"That's a real pool cue," he replied with a Cheshire grin. He used his real cue to push imaginary balls into her pocket.

She was surprised that Timmy's cue was so small and that it didn't have any hair. He had commented on the hair that surrounded her bumper. That had embarrassed her. For years since, she has tried to pull it out so that she would be as smooth as she remembered Timmy's cue.

Marilyn enjoyed playing bumperpool with Timmy. Sometimes his father suggested that they play outside with other kids, but Timmy pooh-poohed him. Sometimes Marilyn's mother, who was already too sick to notice much, noticed that Marilyn was spending a lot of time with Timmy; she thought it was nice that Marilyn had such a good friend. She knew that Marilyn didn't fit in that well with the other children. Her mother told Marilyn to cherish Timmy Wang because good friends were hard to find.

Marilyn, thinking of Timmy Wang's real cue getting hard and pushing past her bumper with its imaginary balls, agreed.

One day, while her mother was still dying, Marilyn's father asked her what she and Timmy liked to do. She told him about playing bumperpool and explained how to play with pants and without pants. Marilyn was rushed to the doctor who insisted on looking inside her pocket. She figured that he was looking to see if Timmy had left any balls inside and then that he was looking to see if there had been splinters from Timmy's cue. She knew there couldn't be, because she knew how smooth it had been. Mostly, she didn't understand why everybody was in such a rush to look where they had never looked before.

The doctor told her parents that she looked red and sore, which Marilyn already knew. He said that she should take long warm sitz baths in Epsom salts and that she should wear mittens at night so she couldn't pull at her hair in her sleep.

But sleep wasn't when Marilyn would pull her hair. That, she did during the day – during the day when she sat thinking about Timmy Wang. She didn't know where the Wangs had moved; she only knew that they had left town shortly after she had told her father about bumperpool. She would think of Timmy Wang, and she would miss him. It was then, in her loneliness that Marilyn pulled at her hair and wondered. She wondered if he missed her. She wondered if they would ever meet again. She wondered if Wang Po had opened a restaurant or a Laundromat. But mostly – mostly she wondered why bumperpool had been so wonderful a game.

Marilyn had missed her friend, Timmy Wang. She hadn't liked Susie O'Neil, whose parents had bought the variety store. She hadn't liked Susie O'Neil because she wasn't Timmy Wang. And once she heard that Mr. O'Neil had gotten a steal. Marilyn didn't know what that meant, but she knew it was wrong to steal, so she disliked Susie even more. But that didn't bring Timmy Wang back.

***

Sometimes Marilyn can hear Old Man Tom screaming in the hallway by her room. Mostly he screams and it means nothing. Sometimes, he screams his dirty words at her. "Cunt, bitch, whore," Old Man Tom calls her in his raspy old man voice. Then Marilyn thinks about playing bumperpool with Timmy and wishes that she could pull the hair which now grows so thick because she no longer can make her hands move.

No one ever mentioned the hair again. It wasn't something you talked about. Marilyn knows that there are lots of things you aren't supposed to talk about: bumperpool and hair were two of them. Sometimes she wishes that Old Man Tom would talk about the hair, but she knows that he won't; she knows that bald men shouldn't talk about hair. She has seen him and knows that he is bald. She thinks it is too bad that she can't give Old Man Tom the hair that she doesn't want. She wonders if he thinks so, too.

Sometimes, long ago, instead of pulling out her hair, Marilyn had played with the lips of her pocket. That would excite her, and she would think about Timmy Wang who had gone away and she would think about the boys in her school. One night when she was playing and feeling excited, she noticed blood. Having no mother, she called her aunt who told her she had become a woman and showed her how to shove a tampon into herself to stop the blood. The next morning she told her father that she had become a woman; he slapped her face, and she knew that she had found something else about which she mustn't speak.

There were so many ways one must not speak; it was better if Rosie spoke. "Speak, Rosie, speak." The silence is cacophonous.

***

Her father had not liked Marilyn becoming a woman; he no longer seemed to like her. The nights passed, and he did not come into her bed. She was glad; she was sad. She was lonely, but she had always been lonely.

It had scared her that she would touch herself and make herself think about boys with pool cues and wanting them inside her. It had scared her because she had known how upset her father had been when she and Timmy Wang had played bumperpool. It had scared her because she had known how much her father had loved to play bumperpool. It had scared her because he no longer came in the night, because he no longer wanted to play – that he no longer loved her.

It scared Marilyn to be a woman. She would stuff a pillow between her legs to keep her hands away – away from secrets and truths she did not understand. Some nights she would writhe about with the pillow between her legs. She would imagine the boys and get excited just as if she were using her hands, just as if they were using their pool cues, the soft ones that they kept hidden – hidden between their legs – and the hard ones, the ones like her father's. But that, too, was something about which she knew she must not speak.

Marilyn hopes that Timmy still plays with his cue and that he remembers her. She hopes that the other boys think about her. She wonders if the other girls think about boys, if they have ever played bumperpool with no pants, if they have ever tried to pull out the hair around their pockets, if they have become women. There are always so many things to wonder about and so few answers.

At least now – now, she knows where to look for the answers. There they are – there inside the plaster, inside the crack, the crack opposite her bed. She hates to be stuck in the dayroom – stuck, helpless, straining – straining in her mind – straining without muscles or movement – straining against the geri-chair – straining to return to the world – her world, the world she shares with Timmy Wang, with Rosie, with the brass band.

Some of the other restrained people like to make believe there is someplace they need to go. They rock and bang their chairs against the wall, and they scream to be let out. Marilyn knows that screaming won't help. She knows that rocking and banging won't help. Other patients, patients who are free to move about, walk back and forth, up and down, like they are in a hurry to be somewhere. But Marilyn knows that they have nowhere to go; she knows that walking back and forth won't help.

She sits snared in her chair and waits in the middle of her silent cacophony. She must wait as Old Man Tom ticks the minutes with his screams. She must wait while the nurses and aides tock the hours with their medications. She must wait until they have decided it is over.

When it is over, when they have decided that the game of bumperpool that isn't real bumperpool has ended, then they will return her to her bed. There is nothing else for her to do but to wait until she can return, until she is returned to the world that really is.

That is how you play bumperpool, waiting until something rolls you past the bumper and into the hole. That much, at least, she understands. She knows how to be a good pool ball.

CHAPTER EIGHT

Buford's education had been the product of a suicide. That is his guilt. He has carried it from the working class suburb where his father, long distanced from the earlier Abrose family's Yankee wealth – wealth accumulated on the flogged backs of kidnapped Africans, had sat in the endless mire of his depression. Buford carried that guilt to the upper-class boarding school, where he had never fit in. He carried it to Princeton, with its eating clubs from which he had excluded himself, and from there to medical school, where he had preferred the company of cadavers to that of humans. He carried it, and it carried him – swept him along to psychiatry, to some unstated pledge that he would be a savior, that he would not allow others to destroy themselves. Or, at least, that if they must end their lives, they would do so without dragging some poor, unsuspecting accomplice into the morass of walls, endless stared-at walls, paint-peeling walls, walls of working class homes from which no laughter could echo, black-hole homes that had lost their humanity.

He is the youngest child, a late and accidental addition. His sister and two brothers were already finished high school when the suicide wheeled his motorcycle in front of Buford's father's screaming semi, that Peterbuild semi rushing through the California hills with its load of furniture – rushing to bring chairs and tables, beds and sofas for track homes that would fill with underpaid engineers and their dreams. His siblings' lives had already been set when the lawsuit had finally been settled. It took a long time, because nobody wanted to blame the dead; nobody wanted to make a claim against the little that was left of him rubbed out, as it were, along the road. And his insurance company didn't want to part with their dollars, not for the traumatized now-ex-truck driver moldering in front of his television with his whiskey of forgetfulness at the ready.

The suit had eventually been settled, but the money had not rescued Jack Abrose from his depression; it had not dispersed the pall, the smog of emptiness, which had settled over the Abrose house. It had given no one happiness or even respite.

Buford, like his siblings, still returns home when necessary, but these are grudging visits based on loyalty to what had once perhaps been, memories of moments that had possibly occurred, moments that had been recalled for depositions, depositions that led to buzzed discussions among lawyers, discussions that ended in Buford's unhappy years at Chumsfield.

The worst part had been his siblings' resentment. Trapped in their roles, they never understood that Buford had been lured into an even more desperate corner. He had flopped about – a desperate fish out of water – trying to find meaning in worlds to which he did not belong. Wealthy scions of long-dead Yankees and Confederates, successful, unguilted descendants of Mayflower and revolution, his classmates wanted nothing to do with a nobody, especially one from a family that had so fallen from grace – unless, perhaps, that nobody could win football games. Possibly if he had been a good quarterback, he might have been accepted – even a lacrosse star. But a non-athletic scholar, reticent, diffident, unknowledgeable of proper etiquette, never having been to Europe, never having been served by a butler: Buford and those who might be like him were not welcome.

But Buford soldiered on, the cross of that suicidal motorcyclist borne on his slight, unathletic shoulders. He accepted the taunts of his schoolmates, the snide comments of the masters, the sneering looks of the masters' wives. He shouldered on and did not allow himself to yearn for home, a place of empty darkness. He did, however, yearn for the remembered past – a world of happier times, of joy-filled memories, a past that had never been except in his desires. He yearned, and, in his yearning, Buford cursed that young man who had so deliberately used his hard-working, loving father, who really wasn't a success or a good father, to end his own life – a life that sounded, from what Buford's family had been told, full of potential.

Buford believed, in some unlit corner of his childhood mind, that he should have prevented the calamity that had darkened his father's soul forever. Perhaps it had been a childish unkind word, an unsaid prayer, a thoughtless act; Buford had not been able to say. But he was sure that had he been a better person God would not have allowed that young man to do this, – not to his father, not to the loving man who would return from each week's work with some simple present, always bought at the same last rest stop, to show, at his wife's demand, that he had held Buford in his heart the entire time that he had driven the long roads.

There had been no present, no trinket on that last day. Jack Abrose had not yet delivered his loads of furnishings when that motorcycle pulled so deliberately under his wheels. He had not yet finished the first cup of coffee of the day's run, that first sugar-laden attempt to push himself through the day.

So, on that last trip there had been no presents, an omission that made Buford all the more sure that somehow he was at fault. Thus, from nothing guilt was born, and so, guilt was borne.

CHAPTER NINE

I am sitting across the beat -up, gunmetal gray desk from him. This new resident, this Buford Abrose, has started like all the others, determined to interview and assess each patient, each inmate, each crazy, to find cures where none have been found before. Diagnoses will be changed. New medications will be tried. Copious notes will be written. It will all end up the same. It always has and it always will. We know, the staff know, the administrators know, even the maintenance and food workers know. He is the only one who does not know.

I am doing my act. I don't know that I could be doing otherwise. I cry. I blame. I talk about unremitting terror. I shake. And I cry some more.

"Do you ever think of killing yourself?" he asks in a soothing voice. It is not clear if this is his suggestion, his concern, or even his own wish.

I go into the cued part of my routine. I cry more profusely and shake more violently. "God, no," I reply between sobs, "I'd be too frightened." I look toward him for the reassurance that I know will come. Sympathy is one of the best forms of attention. It means that I will be able to get what I want from him, that I will be able to get privileges: opportunities to leave the ward, possibly even day passes – the little reinforcements of madness. It means that he will be hesitant – at least until he learns who handles the whip – to up my medication at the whim of the nurses and the aides. Sympathy and cigarettes are the two currencies of any asylum.

A chain smoker, I use any cancer sticks that come my way – any brand, any condition – fresh from the pack, partially smoked, butts from the ground. Hell, I'll even clean the bathrooms for three cigarettes. That's the worst job to get; everyone hates it. Everyone knows that I am too much a nicotine addict to turn them down. Three smokes and I'm up to my pits in shit. I'd charge more if I could, but nobody ever has more. Butts go as fast as a house on fire.

He smiles wanly at me. This new doctor wants to help, but in that smile I see his weakness. He is clearly weak, too weak to withstand the forces that will swirl around him, those dark forces that in the end make us all, inmates and staff, into a Bedlam from which few of us will ever escape. Part of me wants at that moment to stop, to reassure him, to tell him not to care, to tell him to run for his own safety – for his own sanity.

But I cannot. Self-interest always trumps altruism, especially in the world of the mad. I half smile in response. It is the kind of washed-out smile that calls for pity. "Don't worry," he tries to reassure me. "I'll take care of those fears. There are some really grand new medications."

I know that it will be a long time before those medications would be available in a state hospital, but I say, "That's great." We are off and running in another game of blind psychiatrist's bluff.

CHAPTER TEN

Buford Abrose is trying to learn the ways of the hospital. He had expected that to be the easy part of his residency. Dealing with severely disturbed patients, patients who were unresponsive to medications, patients for whom release into the community either would never come or would quickly fail: that he had expected to be the hard but interesting part. He had been wrong. There seemed to be an endless array of petty rules and even pettier norms, and they seemed to consume his time and determine his mood.

Jennifer Teraso, R.N., is just now taking him to task. As head nurse of the entire hospital she lords it over the first year residents with sadistic relish, and they have no choice but to accept it. Without her there is no way to master the endless rules and administrative requirements, most of which exist only in and for her and Dr. Partles's minds.

"I'm sorry. I really don't understand."

"I thought you completed medical school and a year of internship." Her nature is, as usual, scathing. Her venom-filled eyes lie hooded and seemingly unblinking behind thick, rimless glasses; her preternaturally black hair seems a direct serpentine gift from Medussa.

Buford thinks about trying to explain that they had done things differently elsewhere, but he knows that for Jennifer Teraso, R.N., and resident cobra, there is no elsewhere. "I'm not sure what...," he begins.

"Never refer to a staff member by name around patients."

"I don't understand."

"God, residents." She sighs for the tenth time during their brief encounter. "You told Michelle that Mrs. Whittle had noticed that she looked a bit shaky."

"She did."

"I know she did. Of course, she did." Her tone is getting even more exasperated. "A good nurse notices those things."

"So what's the problem?"

"You should have said, 'nurse noticed that you look a little shaky.'"

"Why?" Unconsciously, he is scratching his left forearm. That had been where he had had poison ivy during the spring. It no longer itches, but under stress he still scratches. This morning he notices it is looking a bit raw. He wonders why, but dismisses it as a scrape. Tomorrow morning, he will notice it has gotten even worse, but he still won't know why.

"That way they can pester."

"Pester?"

"Ask 'Why did you say that?' You know, bother us."

Nurse Teraso stares at Buford – waiting for and not expecting to see comprehension. With a snort of exasperation she continues, "If 'nurse' said it, they don't know whom to bother."

"Rightttt." Buford's tone makes both his uncertainty and dawning comprehension audible. He pauses for a moment and then asks, "Won't they bother everybody?"

"No, they get too confused."

He thinks that is a strange goal, to confuse the patients in a psychiatric hospital. On the other hand, he has been at the hospital for a week and has only been getting more and more confused himself.

The other first year residents have arrived. The older residents are there. The attendings are there. The director of training is also back - from a trip to Europe, which the third year residents whisper was really a trip to the funny farm. Dr. Virgil Bartholemu is neither noted for his emotional stability nor for his professional acumen. He is, however, noted for his compliance. In the state system compliance is considered an important qualification. He stands next to Nurse Jennifer Teraso shaking his head in agreement.

"So it's 'nurse said', 'doctor said', 'aide said'?"

"No, the aides have names. They're Mr. or Mrs. so and so."

"What about Miss? Are the women all married?" He has thought that he is learning. He is, once again, wrong.

"We refer to them as Mrs. anyway. It keeps the men under better control," Dr. Bartholemu contributes in his whiny voice. The nurse glares at him. She wants no interference, even if it is intended to support her. She knows that this useless physician, this cousin of the wife of a past state superintendent of mental health, who will soon return to the office in which he hides so assiduously – she knows, everyone knows, that Wayne Bartholemu only comes onto the wards when it is absolutely necessary, when, for instance, he has to escort a new resident – that is, after all, a part of his job, a requirement with which he is expected to comply. Of course, Buford has already started his duties, but protocol has to be served. So here he is, trying to make it sound like he knows something, anything. And the nurse who really captains this sinking ship wants him gone – disappeared, before Buford or anyone else might get the mistaken idea – the idea that has been papered into place by the government and that has no reality – the idea that anyone but she, especially anyone like Wayne simpering-fool Bartholemu, is in charge.

In his head, Dr. Bartholemu reassures himself that this trip through purgatory will soon end, that he will return quickly to his office where his secretary will shelter him from not only his duties but also from the outside world. There he will sip tea and read newspapers until lunchtime. Then, he will play golf, enough holes to justify his visit to the nineteenth hole. That is the goal of his day: the bar where he will sit drinking until his wife comes to find him and pour him back into the appearance of normality.

"And the patients?" Buford asks.

"First names. If they have the same first name, use the first name and the initial. 'Tom S, I want to see you for medication.' Understood?"

"I guess so, but doesn't it make the patients feel like they're, I don't know, something less?"

The nurse sighs loudly and then turns the full force of her angry gaze on him. "Aren't they?"

CHAPTER ELEVEN

They walk into Marilyn's room. They don't knock; nobody ever does. The door is open as it almost always is. It doesn't matter. Privacy doesn't matter, not in the asylum – more importantly, not for her, not in their world. For Marilyn, the world in which she lives, that world is private. It lies beyond them, in another universe, one from which they are excluded. Her will makes it so. Over that alone she has complete control.

Marilyn doesn't recognize them. If she could have, she wouldn't have wanted to anyway. She tries her hardest to never recognize. Recognition means acknowledgement; acknowledgement means accepting their presence, the existence of their world. Marilyn's world is there – there inside the crack in the wall – inside the crack into which she stares whenever she is left to do so, whenever she is left to be free.

"I'm Dr. Partles. I'm the administrative director of the hospital. This is Dr. Abrose. He's going to be your therapist."

Doctor Particles" she thinks. *I've never seen a doctor in particles.* She imagines him disintegrating. She wishes him into tiny pieces; she wishes him away – away, away from her, away from Timmy Wang, away from her crack, away from her world.

Wonder of wonders, horor of horors, he doesn't disintegrate; he does, however, leave. But the other one, the one made not of roses but – appearing almost translucent in the morning light - is perhaps of flawed amber, walks across the room and sits in the green leatherette chair with its chrome frame. It isn't like the chairs she is strapped in when she is wheeled out of her room to play bumperpool with the world. He can get up whenever he wants to. *Why,* she wonders, *why would anybody want to get up? For that matter, why would they sit, or lie, or anything? It is better, so much better, to not – to not stand, sit, lie, or, most importantly, be. To be or not to be, what an easy choice. What a peaceful, easy choice.*

The doctor of yellow light gets up and re-crosses the room to close the door. "We wouldn't want anyone listening."

Why not? she wonders. *What's he going to say that no one should hear?* It doesn't matter. Marilyn has done all the listening she has ever wanted to do anyway. She has listened through doors and around corners, and what has that gotten her?

He walks back to the green chair with the chrome frame. She notices that he has a slight limp favoring his left foot. That is a good sign. People who limp can't run as fast. She could run away – away into the crack. There she would find safety – there, in the world of Timmy Wang, there in the world of brass bands. She would hide in the gazebo where everyone could see her, everyone but this one, this strange doctor who wants to sit in the green leatherette chair.

He squirms himself into the chair. It isn't a comfortable chair. Marilyn has never sat in it, but she had seen Celeste urinate on it one day. Celeste had taken down her pants and squatted on the chair. As the urine dripped down the chrome legs, aides had come running to take Celeste away.

***

Marilyn had wet herself once. It had been years ago when she was a little girl inside another wall. She had been in kindergarten and had been too excited playing duck, duck, goose to raise her hand and tell the teacher that she needed to make. She had squatted down on the mat they used for play, and everyone laughed and said "oh," just as if she had done something very special. She hadn't felt special, just relieved – relieved and wet. When her sickly mother came with dry clothes and a scowl, Marilyn said that she was sorry, but she really didn't understand why she should be sorry when everybody had said oh just as if she had done something very special. She didn't understand why she should be sorry that she was wet. She promised not to do it again so the next time she had to go peepee she hid behind the play kitchen and nobody knew. There she had made the puddle that the teacher cleaned up while everybody sat quietly in a circle.

"Good boys and girls go in the toilet," the teacher had said. Marilyn hadn't said anything. The next time that she had to urinate at school, she went in her pants and said nothing. Not knowing what else to do, she had just stayed wet and waited to go home. After that she tried not to go peepee in school. She wanted to be a good little girl, but she wasn't sure what a toilet was. Maybe if the teacher had said "bathroom" or "potty", then Marilyn would have understood, but no one at home ever used the word toilet.

Since she has come to the hospital, Marilyn wets herself constantly, soils herself, too, but that doesn't matter because she is again a very little girl whose diapers are changed. Sometimes the changing is done with great care, and it makes Marilyn feel that she is loved – that she has been a good girl, that she is special. Sometimes her diapers are changed roughly. Then she knows that she has been naughty, but it is okay to be naughty here. Except – except, she is so afraid of being naughty. She is particularly afraid to be bad when John is around. She knows that he hates her, that he wants to hurt her. He is so rough when he changes her diaper that she trembles inside herself after he has left the room.

**

So the unparticled amber doctor sits on the cleaned off urine that Celeste had given Marilyn, and Marilyn wonders if he feels wet. She hopes that he does because he has no business sitting in her room and staring at her – staring at her as if he could see her playing bumperpool with Tommy Wang, staring at her as if he could see the big cancer worm that had eaten her mother, staring at her as if he were Rosie waiting for her to throw a stick. If she had wanted to speak, Marilyn would have told him to go away. But she never wants to speak. Instead, she thinks about a river of urine. She imagines him being carried away in the yellow stream – being cleansed away to a place that never was, that never would be.

Timmy Wang had made streams of urine. He had liked to take his clothes off, stand on a rock and pee and make boy streams. Sometimes Marilyn climbed on top of the rock and squatted and peed, too. But she couldn't make streams that could carry away doctors made of particles or amber or much of anything. Instead, it would splash in all directions.

She wishes a rushing river of urine to carry the doctor and the green chair with its chrome frame far away. Wishing doesn't work, so she wets the bed. Over that she has control. She squeezes as hard as she can until the peepee spills out of the edges of her diaper, until he notices.

He does notice. She can see his nose move in response to the fish-like odor of her urine. Inside she laughs at his discomfort; outside she is wet. It is the wetness of the five-year-old giggling girl hiding behind the make-believe refrigerator. It is the wetness of the rock bearing witness to Timmy Wang's wong. It is the wetness of her wish that her wishes could make themselves real.

Dr. Buford Abrose carefully makes a note on the lined yellow pad he has been carrying. He uses the gold pen which his wife had given him when he graduated from medical school a year earlier. He pauses for one moment before he actually writes. It seems strange to be using such an expensive instrument for this first clinical note: The patient appears to have wet herself. Is incontinence a problem or was this a reaction to my presence?

Perhaps I should buy some BIC pens, he thinks. *I should save this pen for private practice, for patients who will be impressed.* He fiddles with the pen for a moment while the odor of Marilyn's urine fills his nostrils. There is a fetid quality to it. Perhaps it is from the medications or perhaps just the lifelessness of her life. He feels nausea and wonders if he will be able to stay in the room for the forty-five minutes, which is her allotted therapy time. Glancing down at his watch, he notes that ten minutes have passed. It seems like time has been standing still. He closes his eyes and breathes through his mouth.

Buford lasts another seven minutes. That is enough – more than he can stand. *We get what we get*, he says to himself as he leaves the room, *and we shouldn't be upset.* He had learned that saying in kindergarten and hadn't thought of it since first grade until now.

Unthinking, Buford closes the door behind him, which guarantees Marilyn an afternoon of respite. In the silence of her personal cacophony, Marilyn is happy. She has wished them away and they have left. Better, they have left her door closed. The joy of solitude rang its bells of appreciation about her head. The wetness does not seem so bad; it had been a good trade. Even the diaper rash that she will surely suffer seems unimportant as she turns her attention to that all-important crack.

CHAPTER TWELVE

Bobby hates doors. He has to be dragged through them. If we go out for recreation, one of the aides stands behind and pushes while another pulls one of his arms. When he has to go to the john, he enlists two of us to help get him into the bathroom. Usually we forget where we've put him. Some days Bobby spends hours in the smelly lavatory until somebody else needs to go and finds him standing facing the wall, head leaning forward against it.

The doctors are convinced that Bobby is afraid of transitions, that he fears change. "Some people are afraid of going over bridges," a staff psychologist had opined at one of the periodic case conferences about Bobby.

"Change can be terrifying if you don't have the mental resources," another doctor responded.

Nobody ever asked Bobby why he feared doorways. One morning when he had been particularly reluctant to go from the bedroom into the hallway through a door that represented no change at all – for none of us were going anywhere anyway – when it had taken four of us to push and pull his mental burdens through that half-broken oft-defaced door, Bobby told us about his fear.

It had happened when he was ten. His parents, much against his wishes, sent him to sleep away camp. Their friend's son had gone to the camp for two years. Their friend's daughters had gone to the camp for one year. They all loved it. Surely, Bobby would have a great time, too.

Bobby said no; his parents said yes. The ping-pong words went back and forth.

"If you're not happy at visiting day, we'll take you home."

"I won't be happy."

"Of course you will."

"No, I won't."

"We'll see."

Bobby reluctantly got on the bus that would take him upstate and to his misery.

Visiting weekend came. Bobby's parents joined the mass of self-satisfied parental humanity that honked its way to the mountains. Bobby met them with, "I want to go home."

"We'll talk about that later. First show us around."

"I hate it here."

"We want to meet your counselors. We want to know how you're doing."

"I'm doing lousy and I want to go home."

"We'll talk about that later."

Bobby's parents were good at ping-pong.

The weekend moved ahead towards the inevitable. Bobby's parents grinned their way through it. Every serve was returned; every volley ended in nothing.

Sunday afternoon came. It was time for parents to leave. Miserable Bobby and unyielding parents stood in the cabin doorway. "You're going to love the rest of the summer," said Bobby's father, hitting him playfully in the arm.

"No, I'm not. I want to go home," responded Bobby, as he hit his father – not so playfully – back.

The force of Bobby's punch had surprised his father, who fell out of the door, landing on a rock and breaking his collarbone.

"He's getting dangerous," Bobby's parents told their general practitioner while Bobby was still being miserable in the middle of the mountains. "He's getting too big for us to handle," they insisted.

From sleep away camp Bobby went on to his first hospitalization. It hadn't done any good, but neither had camp. He was, however, happier at the hospital. At least the door to the ward was locked; that kept his parents out. That meant that he couldn't hurt them. Locked doors make good parents.

CHAPTER THIRTEEN

Marilyn had always enjoyed Celeste's visits, at least as much as Marilyn could enjoy anything. Celeste would sit rocking back and forth and rubbing her hands together while Marilyn would think about the world beyond the crack in her wall. Celeste wasn't scary because she always had so many smells and sounds. People with smells and sounds can't sneak up on you. Celeste never sneaked up on anyone – at least, no one other than Celeste. She had wanted to be noticed.

Marilyn isn't sure if the un-leaving amber doctor, who has again squirmed into the Celeste-soaked chair, wants to be noticed or not. She only knows that she wants him to not notice her.

"If I hide behind the big tree, they won't see me."

"If I hide in that bush, they'll go by."

"If I stay under my bed, no one will notice."

The little girl is playing hide-and-go-seek. There are boys looking for her – for her hiding in the gazebo and trying to look like a tuba.

All the boys look like Timmy Wang and they carry long snakes that undulate in the air with their long tongues poking this way and that, their long tongues with so many eyes darting through her safety.

She is hiding, and she is hoping, oh, so much, that they will find her.

They do! They find her! It is delicious to be found. It is exciting to be discovered.

The excitement sets off another burst of urine. The doctor opens his eyes, makes another note on his pad. He looks at his watch. Unmoving time has again passed.

"I think we've had enough for today's session. I'll see you tomorrow." His voice is measured. He speaks respectfully to the air.

It is John who comes to give her a sponge bath and change her. She doesn't like the roughness of his hands as he scrubs away her urine and rolls her body to change the bed.

He doesn't like her wetness or her smell. He resents the task. He despises her. His roughness gives him pleasure.

John leaves.

Marilyn thinks that a nurse should come and look for splinters. This time she is sure there would be some.

CHAPTER FOURTEEN

Stan and I would take long bike rides. They were accompanied by a strange mixture of feelings. On the one hand, there was the exhilaration, a combination of nine parts freedom and one part physical exertion. On the other, there was fear. Not the crazy fear that eventually came to haunt me, but the realistic fear that came from being minority members in a cruelly prejudiced town.

We would ride furiously until we were out of the city limits. Greater Boston was a jigsaw puzzle of ethnic and religious neighborhoods. Once out of one city and across the border into the next, the mix of people would change. Suddenly, the helpless prey were no longer powerless, and the predators were to be hunted.

Most of the time, we made our exit successfully. Sometimes, we had a desperate race to reach the line that would demark safety. On a couple of occasions we were caught and paid the price in black and blue, cigarette burns, and kicked bicycles. Then we would walk the long walk of shame with lopsided wheels furiously weaving and veering and smaller kids laughing and jeering.

It is ironic to look back and to realize that Stan was the far more cautious bike rider. At that point in my life I felt indestructible. Or at least I dwelled within a fantasy of indestructibility, a science fiction fantasy of having been stolen from my rightful parents who lived on a distant planet, parents of wealth and unimaginable super-powers.

Jack has never outgrown that kind of delusion. If determination can make it so, he will eventually lead his great revolution and eventually take over the world. Today he is creating his cabinet. He has offered me the ministry of the army. I indulge him with the humor that his unintended irony deserves. An army run by a coward might in fact be a good thing, for it would be afraid to fight. Ah, but what if he discovers that he doesn't need to fight, that he can send others to battle? Such a minister might be all the more ready for war – to let the deaths of others be his compensation for his own terror. Perhaps, though my acquiescence is in jest, perhaps I should tender my resignation.

Jack is what passes for my best friend on the ward. He considers himself God's prophet and the hope of mankind. I won't say that he thinks he's the Christ, but if western religions accepted avatars, I'm sure he'd at least be John the Baptist. In Jack's faith, however, there would be much more debauchery and good living. There would probably be some heavy drug use, too. I know that he's planning to legalize it all when he takes over Australia. I asked him once about all the bad things he wanted to do. He laughed and told me it was God's plan. In Jack's cosmology, God needs something to do. Fighting evil is His job. Stop the evil, and God would die. "It was bad enough that the Jews killed Christ," he says, ignoring my ethnicity. "I'm sure as hell not going to kill off God, too."

To be honest, I always figured that God was killed off at Auschwitz, but I'm not going to argue theology with a guy who thinks he's a prophet.

Before my tracheotomy I would sometimes argue with Jack about other things. Now I know better. It's too easy to get noticed here, and a preacher is always one of the first to be condemned. We walk up and down the dayroom and discuss his judgments and his plans. I agree with everything. Hopefully, he will never come to power, but nobody ever expected Hitler to make it, and look what his madness accomplished. Nobody expected Mao to make his long march, but he and his little cohort took over all those Chinamen. Madmen have an unusual capacity to pursue their dementias, maybe because they don't have to deal with reality – at least not in their heads.

If you use that as the measuring stick of sanity, the awareness of how reality will interfere with your plans, then I have to admit that I'm pretty sane. On the other hand, I really have to question a lot of politicians.

And then, on the always obsessive other hand, if you're too aware of how reality can intrude into your life, how it can crash in on you, how it can destroy you, then life becomes intolerable – too fraught with angst to withstand. Then you end up here, in the asylum with me, or you end up like Stan. Concrete reality gives an end to it all. Go up against a semi and, well, that's an end devoutly to be wished, an end to make cowards of us all.

CHAPTER FIFTEEN

When Stan died, I didn't go to the funeral. I was in college, and my parents didn't want to upset me so they didn't tell me that my cousin and best friend had died, had been killed, had committed suicide. I didn't know that he was dead until I showed up at his parents' home. My uncle was hiding in his lounge of seclusion – painting, no doubt, for the hundredth time, that seascape of his despair. My aunt threw her arms around me and immersed herself in tears. The ululations of her grief still haunt my dreams.

If there is a God, something that I doubt but simultaneously want to believe, I wonder how he could ignore such grief. *Why, I ask myself, didn't He do something to relieve her suffering?* Perhaps it was for the same reason that if He wasn't gassed He still allowed Hitler's holocaust and all the other mass killings of history. Perhaps it's that He simply doesn't care. If God exists, I wonder if He has founded another, more worthy world. Certainly this world and the sadness that man has made in it don't merit divine presence – not unless Jehovah is a sadist.

Mankind may have free will, but we seem bent on making the self-destructive choices. Maybe Stan was the real prophet, self death his real prophecy. Perhaps it is only hubris to believe that we can matter. Perhaps it is also pride to believe that the ones we love will not disappear. Or perhaps it is only delusion, only madness. In that case, there is no asylum, no sanctuary, only the endless gray of the tossing seas of the endless paintings of our endurance.

CHAPTER SIXTEEN

Where does she go? Buford Abrose, M.D., first year resident in psychiatry, and Marilyn's "therapist" squirms in the standard issue chrome, green, and uncomfortable chair and wrestles with his thoughts. It has been three weeks since their first session, three weeks since he had asked Dr. Partles for a new, hopefully more comfortable chair, three weeks during which Marilyn has said not a word.

She had urinated on herself twice during the early sessions. He had interpreted that as a primitive form of communication and made some absurd intellectualized notes with his gold pen – the one his wife had given him, the one that now lies at the bottom of his underwear drawer waiting for patients whose communications were worthy of it. There has been nothing else; in three weeks there has been nothing. The silence upsets Buford, makes him feel inadequate.

He has the strangest feeling as he sits watching Marilyn and beyond her the closed yellow-green door of her room. He feels that she is not here, that she has somehow left, leaving behind an inert physical mass that looks like her but isn't. It isn't like the feeling that haunts him when he visits his parents, the guilt-ridden feeling of staring into the endless maw of his father's depression. It is not the sense of unfathomable darkness. It is the sense of an emptiness, a ghostly emptiness that leads nowhere, that touches nothing.

He tells his supervisor about the feeling. "Where does she go?" he asks the always well-groomed and accessorized Dr. Susan Lavanger. With a lucrative private practice in the city and her not-insubstantial consulting fees from the state, she can afford gold pens and jewelry and expensive clothing. Wrapped as she is in the armor of her grooming, nothing ever seems to faze Dr. Lavanger. In fact, she seems more robotic than human, answering questions with textbook precision and total indifference.

She in not interested in the patients or in the residents whom she supervises. Susan Lavanger is interested in the title of supervisor, she is interested in the certificate which hangs on the wall of her office in the city, and she is interested in the opportunities that title offers for television interviews. She always dresses well but especially for those interviews. She knows that publicity is the sustenance of high fees.

Buford has heard rumors about her, about her sadomasochistic sexual practices, about the clubs in New York where she beats men with riding crops and rides them naked like horses – bareback in perversion. He has heard the rumors, and he has believed them. He believes them enough to fear the day she might bring her whip to bear on him.

"She's catatonic," Dr. Susan Lavanger responds with the cold assurance that labeling something explains it – the assurance that diagnosis can remove a patient's humanity; the assurance that a thing, as opposed to a human, requires no concern, no feeling, no awareness. For Dr. Lavanger, the patients have become objects somewhat less important than filing cabinets and desks, and the residents, like this bumbling idiot with his inane questions, are only a step higher in her mind.

He gives dumb a bad name, she smirks to herself as she glances at the perma-press clad resident with his yellow pad and BIC pen. *Truly a village idiot.* There – a label, a dismissal. Buford relegated. He has taken enough energy. She turns her attention to something important. She thinks about her date of the evening.

There are other catatonic patients in the hospital; Buford has spent some time in their rooms, too. But he hasn't felt the same way. Of course, he hasn't been spending an hour a day, five days a week with them. Two other first year residents have been assigned catatonic patients. He has asked them if they experienced the same absence of the person. They haven't. He doesn't dare mention that to Dr. Lavenger.

"When we find the right medication," she monotones on, "her catatonia will lift. Till then she needs diapering and feeding and an occasional bathing. There's not much point in anything else."

The implication of his own worthlessness stings Buford. He argues back. "I think that it means something to her for me to be there. No matter how primitively she's functioning, she still needs someone."

"A dependable object?" He can see by the set of her mouth that Dr. Lavanger has no faith in psychoanalytic theories and no regard for him. What he can't know is the depth of her scorn. *He needs a good beating*, she says to herself. *Definitely a good beating. Not worth riding – or fucking – too cheap looking. But a beating, that would do him some good.*

"Something like that."

"Well, I don't see that you can do her any harm," is her spoken response. *Asshole* has been reserved for her own hearing.

Buford knows that he isn't going to get any more support than that lukewarm endorsement, so he changes the subject. His supervisor is far more willing to discuss the medical dangers of the pigeon shit that is layering ever higher on the porches of the long-out-of-date red-brick hospital buildings.

He had learned long ago that life is filled with promises and disappointments. His first lesson had been as a child, a child whose father was a hero who drove big rigs, a knight of the road. Even then, nothing was as it advertised.

CHAPTER SEVENTEEN

Sitting in Marilyn's room, Buford often experiences extreme, even existential, loneliness, a coldness that grips his soul as if in the presence of evil – not simply badness but primordial evil, the evil of the devil. The early sessions, when Marilyn had wet herself, had been physically discomforting, but the coldness he now so often experiences speaks to his sense of human destiny.

I wonder how I'd feel if I knew that I was the last person left on earth. Would I try to survive, or would I commit suicide? He sits in his chrome and green discomfort and contemplates the question. It seems to him that he would probably start out trying to survive and then eventually, like a rock in the face of a small but unrelenting stream, give in to the desperation of despair.

Despair, the absence of hope. To be away from the Spirit. He knows that the rationalism of psychiatry would frown on his religious interpretation. Yet, he wonders if the absence of God is not the essence of such a sense of absolute loneliness.

In the absence of communication, Marilyn is forcing Buford to think very deeply. He stirs uncomfortably in the chair.

What was that joke? He tries to remind himself. It had been a bit racist, and he had rejected it at the time, but now he needs something to laugh at.

There was a psychiatrist who gave a costume party every year.

That's it. He remembers the joke.

His patients would come dressed as an emotion, and he, the psychiatrist, would guess which emotion they represented. He went into the first room, there was a man dressed in red with a pitchfork. You're anger, said the psychiatrist.

That's wonderful, said the man. 'How did you know?

That's easy. I've been doing this for years.

The next patient was a woman wearing a slinky black, low cut dress. You're sexy, said the psychiatrist.

That's wonderful, said the woman. How did you know?

That's easy. I've been doing this for years.

The next patient was a nude black man. His only costume – the only thing he wore – was a pear stuck on the tip of his penis. The psychiatrist looked and thought and thought some more. I give up.

I'm fuckin' dis pear.

Buford wonders if Marilyn is also feeling fuckin' dis pear.

Despair, disrepair, disappear, disappear where? God, I'm beginning to sound hebephrenic. Is that what happens? Does the emptiness of the lives here empty your own? Maybe I'm not cut out for psychiatry. Alice keeps telling me to switch to something that will pay better. What would that be, dermatology? Yeah, something that sits on the surface, nothing too deep – dry the wet and wet the dry – don't go beyond skin-deep. Don't try to get inside someone's head.

His ruminations are suddenly spoken words. "Will you ever let me in? Will you ever let you out? Where are you? For God's sake, where am I?"

He takes out his BIC pen, the one that has replaced the gold that Alice had given him

"I really ought to get some more pens." He says it aloud with anger, as if it were the pen that is stopping him from writing. In reality, he needs to hear his voice filling the void, echoing against the fuckin' dis pear.

It is the fifteenth hour of what might laughingly be called their work together. He feels there ought to be something, something more significant on the page than what he finally writes: No change today.

Buford continues to stare at his yellow pad. He turns the page and stares at the empty yellow paper with its faintly green lines. Finally, he draws a picture. He isn't sure where the idea comes from. It is a picture of a tree and a dog digging under the tree for some unknown object. He isn't very talented or artistic. The drawing looks like something from a junior high school art class. He tears the sheet off and crumples it. There is no wastebasket in the room so he stuffs the crumpled sheet into his jacket pocket. It makes a bulge in the already ill-fitting white jacket that defines him as a doctor.

Buford looks down at the pad again. He has still not found the right words. Then he writes:

Once I was lonely,
Mommy's away.
I wish I had someone
With me to play.
I thought that I knew
So much about life;
I know I was wrong,
But I don't have any idea what comes next.

What the hell? he thinks. He looks at his watch. He is getting very good at judging forty-five minutes. "Today is Friday," he says. "I'll see you again on Monday. That will be in three days." He wonders if he is pretending at being a grown-up speaking to a child for Marilyn's sake or for his own.

CHAPTER EIGHTEEN

Jack is thin, painfully thin. With his bent posture and gawky long neck, arms, and legs, he looks almost frail. Yet his muscles are taut. They, like his mind, are a mass of coiled springs ready to be set in motion in every direction by the slightest stimulation. His body belies the carbohydrate diet, the medications, and the lack of exercise that have made most of us at best pudgy and at worst physical disasters.

His head is far too large for his frame. When he walks, he bends forward so that his cranium seems to be pulling the rest of his body along. His eyes are light blue, almost a diamond blue, piercing, and betray the intensity of his pathology. Those eyes are not so much mirrors of the soul as a window through which to watch the demons of Legion as they churn their wrath.

Each day these demons – his demons – writhing and un-exorcised, seem to demand more and more of Jack's being. Consequently, he has become progressively less available for discussion. Our daily walks up and down the dayroom have ceased to be a chance for conversation. Instead, I am reduced to audience. He rants and I listen. I listen to his hoarse-whispered diatribes, to his raging condemnations.

His anger ranges through the world like a righteous whirlwind, like the Biblical plagues of his imagining. His thoughts leap from the doctors to the government to women to Blacks to the aides to religion to the other patients. Along the way they have something demonic to offer about every group and every ethnicity. Even his beloved Australia – to which he had never been – takes its share of verbal abuse.

For myself, I am tolerated. I am to be his biographer. I am to share his message with the world and to be his Secretary of War. And woe betides me if I were to let him down; the terrors of Trotsky would be nothing compared to the wrath that would pull down on my head. His is an anger that can tolerate no interference, no negation. In his mind his impotence, the medications that are daily forced into him, the barred windows and locked doors that contain us all are but preparations for the day of his judgment.

The ward staff is not unaware of Jack's growing rage. They have tried new medications, but without results. I know that it will only be a matter of time before they will resort to shock or even surgery. I try to warn him. I point to Charlie, poor shuffling Charlie, and remind Jack of what had happened to that once interesting, if erratic, soul. In the throes of his megalomania, Jack cannot hear my warnings. He cannot see the truck with which he is doomed to collide. But then, who among us can?

In his way, Jack is a caricature, a mirror of the society that has produced him. There is the fantasy, dearly held by Americans, that we are a kindly and just people, a people of fairness and of law. I do not know that we are worse than other people, but all our self-descriptive paeans of praise ignore the sadistic bestiality that lies beneath our glittering surface. This is not a kindly place. Stan and I learned that reality by escaping and not escaping from the other boys who would gladly beat us up and burn us with their smokes, who joyously debased us to "teach those dirty kikes a lesson."

Others might say that those experiences were atypical. Fine! Consider the phenomenon of hazing. The histories of college fraternities and clubs are replete with physical and even sexual abuse. Varsity football players sodomize their younger teammates in the name of team solidarity, and the younger footballers in turn try to tyrannize their schoolmates.

We have so many people rotting in our bestial jails, and so many more sleeping in the gutters of our cities. We rape and we murder. Guns are everywhere. Violence is everywhere. This is not a kindly place.

The demons who watch the world through Jack's blue orbs are but a reflection of the capacity for the sadism which they see around him. If all Americans don't want to conquer the earth, there are certainly enough of them who do. Worse, more and more of them are gaining political power. Soon the Jacks will be running the asylums. Perhaps, as I watch the aides once again drag my friend off to the rubber room, perhaps, I muse, they already are.

When I was a child, a terrified child who could not summon up his imagined extraterrestrial parents nor maintain his secret powers against the rage around him, I would construct intricate string fortresses beneath tables or I would take refuge behind sofas or large chairs. Creeping from imaginary fortification to imaginary redoubt, I learned to avoid trouble. I learned that the quiet soldier was not wounded in battle. Sadly, I know that I cannot teach that to Jack. I knew that his prophetic voice will not be stopped by me. If I do not believe his prophecies, I do not want to see him deprived of his capacity to express his sense of outrage against the world. But, in the end – the always bitter end – his voice will be stopped. That is, after all, the responsibility, the goal of the asylum.

Too bad for Jack. Too bad for Charlie. Too bad for me. Too bad for everyone.

CHAPTER NINETEEN

We grow old. There is no way for the living to escape age. It wraps its tentacles around the body and refuses to loose hold. Even the best-lived lives are like a pen, for all the wisdom or the scribbles it may mark, the nib is worn away the same. In his day, Mitch was quite the success. A journalist, he reported from battlefields and corporate headquarters. He revealed the foibles of the wealthy and the chicanery of the powerful. As a professor he had enlightened younger, inquiring minds in a top university. All that had done nothing to keep his brain from gradually disintegrating.

I've been told that his family, his children, tried to keep him at home, but the increasing fits of violence, the fecal finger paintings, and the need for constant supervision had become more than they could handle. Their children needed them, and that had to be the priority. If Mitch had still been able to reason, he would have told them that they were making the right choice.

When his medical insurance ran out, Mitch was relegated to this place of madness. But even here on the edge of purgatory, his children take turns visiting. Every other Sunday, no matter what the weather, one of them shows up. They always bring small packages of the foods that he used to love – figs, fancy cheeses, fine chocolates, and more. While they are here, they push those delicacies into his mouth, and he compliantly swallows without chewing, without tasting. As soon as they leave, the aides confiscate the remainders of the package and one of them takes it home. They take turns taking those packages home. After all, who is there to tell those loving grown children? Certainly not another of the inmates, another mindless creature unable to make sense of the world. What can we, the legion denizens of this mired depth, possibly know of greed? Of lack of care? Compared to the lack of justice in Mitch's dementia, what are a few figs? A few dainties? Nothing. Everything.

We wait for the Mitch in each of us to deteriorate – to start attacking, to smear feces on the walls, to scream into the night. We wait. We know it will come. We've seen it before. We know that there will be a geri-chair – dementia contained like an animal in a tiny cage. With more time and more deterioration there will be another ward – a ward filled with people in geri-chairs, pathetic people full of senility, unable to recognize, unable to care about figs or cheese. Unwitting people, unwitted people, people run down by a different kind of monstrous truck.

I want to ask: Who? What? When? Where? How? Why? I want to cover this story of Mitch's senility, to give it some meaning, some comprehension. How do I interview a neuron? *When did you decide to commit your own little suicide?* I would ask it. I know that it would not answer, that it could not answer. Yet, in my head I hear its voice. *Don't worry! It is painless.*

I know the neuron lies.

CHAPTER TWENTY

"Leprosy, I've got leprosy. There goes my eyeball into your highball." Far away the voices echo and mutter. Marilyn knows that she wants them to go even farther. Fathers come and fathers go. Maybe her father has drowned; she lets go of the overturned boat and dives – a mermaid – to find him. As she dives deeper the voices come startlingly closer and then recede. The only things she can now hear are the parts of Celeste's body falling to the ground. It is safe now. Celeste will make the chair clean. She will wash away the scent of the man who had closed the door and sat in the green chair with the chrome frame. Celeste will urine away the desecration.

But it isn't Celeste. Celeste hasn't ever come back. Instead there is a new chair, big, covered in black fabric. It is a father's chair, stern and angry. It is a chair for a judge. She wonders if she will be on trial. She hopes that she won't be tried for having leprosy. Once, long ago, with her dying mother, who already had the cancer worm eating away her insides, Marilyn had gone to see *Ben Hur*. She remembers what happened to lepers; she doesn't want to live in a cave in a valley. She doesn't want to be thrown, like the garbage, out of life. She does not realize that has already happened.

***

It is a green valley. It is filled with sheep. Rosie is chasing the sheep and barking with joy. "Stupid dog; those aren't foxes."

"Kiss me quick, there goes my upper lip."

"Rosie, help me find Erik."

"Erik drowned. Celeste drowned Erik."

"No, she drowned the chair." It was the judgment. She is terrified. They had dismembered Celeste. They had given her leprosy, and she had fallen apart.

"Rosie, where did you get that hand? Bad dog. You shouldn't be eating that."

"Baa," Rosie bleats.

***

How many judges does it take to give you a leprosy sentence? There are three of them carrying the green chair with the chrome frame out the door. There are three of them who have put the black chair in its place.

There is a trinity, a holy trinity. "Hail, Mary, mother of lepers. Pray for our body parts now and in the time of their transfusion."

"Can't you sing another song?"

"There are songs that make you happy, there are songs that make you sad. There are songs that make you sorry, sorry that you're mad."

"Those aren't the words."

"I can't hear you, my ears fell off."

"Rosie, can you find her ears? No, don't chew them. Put them on the chair so that no one can sit there. That's a chair for listening. I don't want them listening to us."

There are no secrets out there, only inside – inside the wall, inside the crack, inside the eye that is God.

They had always closed their door at night. Once she tried to quietly open it and sneak into their room. Her parents had been close together, holding on to each other. When they heard her, her father jumped away from her mother and yelled at her. The next time she tried to sneak into their room, the door was locked. "Go back to bed, Marilyn," her mother had called.

"Yes, mommy," she had lied. Then she had lain in the hall and tried to listen. She hadn't understood the noises they were making. She heard her mother saying words you weren't supposed to say and her father panting hard like he was digging a ditch. During the day he was a stockbroker; at night he dug ditches in Mommy.

That had been before the cancer worm. That had been before bumperpool. That had been before Daddy had come into her room in the middle of the lonely nights.

Why was it okay for Mommy and Daddy and not for Timmy Wang and Marilyn? She wonders if the judge knows. Had he, too, listened at the door? Was he listening now, listening outside the crack in the wall opposite her bed?

"What happened to my nose? Is there anyone who knows?"

"You've got to stop singing those songs."

"Why?"

"Because everybody will think you're strange."

"Am I strange?"

"Well, yessss, I guess you are. But you don't have to advertise the fact."

It's hard being a stranger. If you tell people your name, what will they do with it? Sometimes they put it on a list. Once you're on a list can you get off? People who make lists have control. People who are on lists have their names "on lists".

It's hard being a not-stranger. Marilyn didn't know how to do that. Her parents wanted her to be one – especially after Erik. They were out in the boat. The motor stopped, and Daddy stood up to start it. The boat tipped over. She almost drowned. Daddy saved her. He didn't save Erik. She didn't understand why Daddy hadn't saved Erik.

She went into the funeral parlor. A boy was lying in a little box. She looked at him, and everyone called him Erik, but it wasn't Erik. Erik jumped up and down and got excited. Erik played rough and tumble and chased Rosie and laughed. It wasn't Erik asleep. When Erik slept, he moved around and made noises and kept you awake. Erik played baseball in his sleep and hit home runs and pitched and caught and won games. It wasn't Erik lying in the box.

She didn't understand where Erik had gone. She didn't understand why they had called what was in the box Erik.

"Leprosy, I've got leprosy. I'm on trial, and the judge is me."

Timmy Wang is lying next to what they called Erik. She knows it is Timmy Wang because she recognizes his pool cue. She wonders what happened to Erik's even littler pool cue when he had drowned. She wants to pull down the pants to see if what they called Erik has a pool cue. Timmy Wang gets up and pulls down her pajamas. He looks for her pocket, but he can't find it. They have sewn it up to keep the cancer worms from getting inside.

The three men are carrying the green chair with the chrome frame out the door. They close the door behind themselves. Marilyn is afraid. Are they going to cover another box? The one in which she is hiding?

She lies as still as she can and watches the body of what they called Erik slowly fall apart. The fingers and toes fall off. His eyes fall out. The flesh fells away from his face. Giant birds come and peck at him. One of the birds is pecking at his pecker. "Shoo," says Marilyn, but nothing hears her.

CHAPTER TWENTY-ONE

Filthy as they are, as in need of repair as they are, I still spend a lot of time in the bathrooms. It isn't a fascination with toilets. It isn't some distortion of sexual energy. I know that's what some of the doctors have thought, but it isn't. It isn't the need for privacy – the privacy of the privy. There's precious little privacy in the hospital. But when I look at asylum life, why would I need privacy? All I possess is my thoughts, and they're as private as I choose to make them. My fantasies are mine; they cannot be taken. And if they were stolen by medication of lobotomy or convulsive therapy or senility – if they were destroyed – why, I wouldn't know they were gone anyway. Then it wouldn't matter.

No, I sit in the bathroom for the smell. It stinks, but it is the stink of bathrooms. It isn't the smell of the psychiatric ward, the smell of human debris, of the pheromonal overload that comes with mental illness, of the years of sweat and tears and fear that have soaked their ways into the institutional walls.

The odor of the bathrooms is, strangely enough, the most normal smell on the ward. It seems that shit is shit, and its smell trumps pheromones every time.

When our ancestors climbed out of their tree nests and wandered the savannah, when they sought shelter in their first caves, they crapped as apes, where and when the urge was felt.

There was no subtlety in their shit, only the remains of fruits and nuts and prey. They preyed then with the same fervor that we pray today – with the same gleeful expectation of happy results.

But shit and caves do not mix well. Ask any epidemiologist and you'll learn about fecal contamination. Of course, if you do, it may take weeks – even months – but a far shorter time than our ancestors took to learn that it's a stupid ape that shits in his own cave.

We humans paid a price for those caves; real estate is always a good investment. We had to learn toilet behavior, we had to get rid of body hair that could trap contaminants – to say nothing of vermin, and we had to lower our awareness of pheromones. How could we have shared such close quarters with so many other potential objects of sex and rage if we didn't learn to mask the incitement, to dampen the excitement? And we had to learn to recognize the smell of feces, to be aware of its presence, to be aware of our own presence. Ultimately, aren't we uniquely an animal aware of its own shit.

I sit in my privy privacy and think about the shittiness of life – my life, everybody's life. I think about the shittiness and I envy Stan. I envy him, and I miss him. God, how I miss him. That's the shittiest thing of all.

CHAPTER TWENTY-TWO

As I sit and smell the reality of my world, my mind wanders in and out of the lives that intertwine with my own. I cannot help wondering what the people who preceded me in this dark place suffered. In the days before phenothiazines and antidepressants, in the days when untreated syphilis attacked so many brains, in the days when these massive red brick buildings were teeming with legions of sufferers, what was life like? I cannot imagine. My mind boggles at the thought of more, of worse, of greater suffering; of more, of worse, of greater dementia. I look at the people around me and sense their pain, and I feel my own. I wonder how our predecessors survived. In a sense, they didn't. They simply died before they were dead. First their minds went, and then – so slowly – their bodies followed until there was naught left to do but lower them into a hole and hold them down with the rich graveyard dirt, the dark worm-crawled dirt that should have grown a garden instead of concealing the twice dead.

It is such a lovely place, this hospital, this asylum, this refuge, this un-holy-day spa. It sits on a point of land that juts into the ocean. Most of the cliffs leading to the water are steep and fierce with weeds and brambles, but there are gentle places where one can reach unused sand beaches, beaches that should in summer be filled with happy bathers, but which are set aside – part of this strangely demented world – for the non-use of the mad. Beaches where the crazed can pace and watch the gentle waves, waves that once hailed graceful three masted vessels and lumbering whalers filled with oil. Beaches where gulls float above and white sands warm the feet below. If only beauty could free the mind. If only rest could end the suffering of the mind.

There are fields, broad expanses of green made for tumbling and running, with occasional full-leafed trees, trees with branches that would invite intrepid young climbers if any were allowed on these grounds. Perhaps once those fields were filled with visitors and staff enjoying the clean, fresh seaside air, but no longer. There are even baselines, backstops, benches, and goal posts; they stand at the slowly-decaying ready for the revelers and athletes who never come, who, if they came, could only shuffle in palsied imitation of sport.

When patients are sufficiently medicated, they are allowed off the wards. Grounds privileges are much prized but only because they mean visits to the little snack bar store where cigarettes, coffee, sodas, and candy bars are available and cheap. Between the charity of visitors and the bits of coin caged from attendants in exchange for washing cars, little chores, and sometimes disjointed sex there is just enough money to keep the store busy.

On weekends and holidays, the patients with grounds privileges line the drives and walks begging from the few overwhelmed visitors. It is a scene from the third world. But we are not in the third world; we are of the fourth – a world outside dimension.

The hospital is its own world occupying a dimension that is separate, a parallel universe in which the normal, the expected, the socially appropriate do not exist. So the patients beg. They prepare themselves for later careers – careers spent at busy intersections, for lives with shopping carts full of worthless possessions, for futures as the castoffs of a society that does not care. This is the vocational training that is offered. The lessons are learned well.

CHAPTER TWENTY-THREE

I watch Jamul lean against one of the decaying brick walls of an empty looming building. He is a rumbling giant of an adolescent. Light cocoa black dressed in black, pitch black, he plays the air-guitar for hours. Usually he doesn't speak – only makes the screech of an electric guitar played by a madman. When he does speak, it is a pastiche of wailed Jimi Hendricks's lyrics.

His forefathers had escaped the chains of slavery. Now he is a slave to some hidden power. It threatens to break free in the music he fails to recreate.

Jamul carries an empty guitar case; he carries it everywhere he goes. Outside, waiting for visitors to come by, it lays open in front of him. Miraculously, people with furtive gazes drop coins. Then they walk hurriedly away. It is not the music that compels them but the guilt. Somehow, great, hulking Jamul reminds them of the sins of their white ancestors. It is a collective guilt shared even by those whose white ancestors came to this world well after the Civil War. It is a sense that somehow things should be different, that Jamul should be wandering free through the forests of Africa. He could not survive there any better than he does in New York. That doesn't matter – guilt is guilt; a few coins for absolution is a cheap price.

He plays his invisible instrument with the wild abandon of musical genius. Another patient, a white boy, another teenager, comes over and leans next to him. The boy mimes opening a case, taking out an imaginary horn, inserting the non-existent mouthpiece, tentatively blowing a few times. Then he becomes a discordant cornet wailing in dissonance with Jamul's guitar. Jamul doesn't notice. Jamul has set his soul on fire.

Unable to distract Jamul, the other boy walks away in hunched back disappointment. No miming in the leaving. Pulling up the overly long pants that sag against a clothesline belt cinched around his artificially bulging belly – no fashion statements here, only castoffs for castoffs. The flotsam of the world, he expects no visitors. He will get no visitors. He will return to his ward and beg the attendants until one, in fatigue and desperation, will either put him in rubber seclusion or allow him the privilege of washing her car for a dollar or a handful of cigarettes.

How many of the workers in a local car wash were thus trained at their state asylum? How many will die hunched over, disappointed deaths?

The hospital is a cruel world disguised as caring, disguised as healing.

A family buys a dog, then they buy a crate for the dog – a cave-like cage for Fido. When they are home, the crate is left open. Fido goes into his cage to sleep, to escape when the children are raucous, to flee when there are angry voices. The cage becomes his sanctuary – his asylum.

What did the hero say? Give me sanctuary or give me death?

Hunched against life we line the entry and scream at those who have not come to visit us. We scream into the storm of life. We scream into the farce of being. We scream: SANCTUARY! SANCTUARY!!! And Jamul plays our accompaniment in twanged chords of desperation.

CHAPTER TWENTY-FOUR

Bobby's parents don't visit – not anymore. Summer camp was long ago. For years they tried to make believe that the hospitals were boarding schools and sleep away camps. They'd make Sunday trips with goodies and games. They'd try to take walks along winding manicured sidewalks that led nowhere. Asylums, like cemeteries, are often well-groomed places. The living want to believe that the dead are enjoying their surroundings.

Gradually, the quality of Bobby's worlds deteriorated as his parents felt the economic strain of their zombie son. Eventually, in the long process of sedimentation, he ended here, ward of the state and bottom of the pile. He had fallen to the earth just as surely as his father had fallen from that camp cabin doorway.

Bobby's father had gotten up from the ground, broken collarbone in agonizing pain. He had gone to the hospital and been slung and medicated. His wife had driven them home. In time he healed. Only the occasional twinge of a rainy day still affected him. He had far more pains and far worse memories from his only son's fall – the fall which nobody could halt, the fall which has ended, at least for now, here, at the mercy of the state.

Bobby doesn't go outside and lean against the walls with the other inmates. Even though he has a grounds pass, he doesn't leave the ward. Even the uncaring aides, the unfeeling overbearing nurses, and the oblivious doctors wish that once, just once, Bobby would let loose the doorjamb and venture into the fresh air. He doesn't.

When the hospital was built, it was placed at the end of the rail line. Perhaps someone thought that rustication might cure madness, but more likely they wanted cheap land for the monumental red brick buildings that marked the graves of the unressurectable.

The need for attendants, cooks, maintenance workers, and the like built the town that now surrounds us. A few commuters use those trains on weekdays, but on weekends there are no travelers at all. The cars are empty. The few visitors who do come drive. Times have long changed. Only madness has not.

Bobby's parents have moved away to a warmer old age. His siblings, if he had had any, might visit, but they, like Jamul's guitar, don't exist and never come. He is alone with the fear of his memories, with the fear of his angry possibilities.

CHAPTER TWENTY-FIVE

It is sundown, and Mitch is sundowning. People with Alzheimer's do that well. No one knows why. Something to do with rhythm: day and night, ovulation and menstruation tango and waltz. Whatever the cause, come sundown they get loonier, more out of control, and generally a hell of a lot more fun or scarier – depending on your connection – then they were earlier in the afternoon.

So Mitch is carrying on. No one does anything about it. The ward is short-staffed, and the people who happen to be on duty are the ones who care the least. They are having some sort of party in one of the offices. Gathered by the door, we can smell the enticing scent of booze. Damn, I want a drink. We all want one – all except Mitch; he is too busy baying at the moon to want anything.

As Mitch's ululations grow in intensity and volume, Charlie becomes agitated. "Oh, boy! Oh, boy! Oh, boy!" he screams without stopping. It provides a counterpoint to Mitch. The coyote and the mastiff battling for control. I wonder if Stan, with his love of jazz, would have approved of this new form of scat. I wonder if he would have joined in, just for the fun of it, for the pure soul releasing, body relaxing joy of it. I try a few tentative yaps and a couple of hesitant yips. Then I let loose with my own visceral full-of-the-moon howl. Three must have been the magic number, for soon everyone has joined in. We are all yowling: lunacy at its finest, madness at its loudest.

***

Orrin Partles, M.D., the administrative director of the hospital, is making his obligatory rounds. He hates leaving his office. He hates it even more than he hates being in his office. But there are certain rules that come ex-cathedra from the state and have to be lip-serviced. True to those regulations, his rounds are not about patient care; we are merely an inconvenience in his preoccupying pursuit, the proper care of the hospital's furnishings. A patient's death, deterioration, or occasional release, these all have simple forms that need to be completed by ward clerks and passed along the chain of command. But the loss of a chair, desk, bed, or filing cabinet requires requisitions – requisitions that appear on budgets, budgets that bring inquiries and questioning.

Mental health is a world of balance sheets, an accountant's paradise in which no outcomes matter and audits can easily be foiled by "patient privacy." "Just keep the paperwork straight" has become his motto, a motto which has served him well over the years of his inevitable rise through the system. He is a system survivor and his motto has served him very well indeed.

Rules and forms have become Orrin Partles' life, his obsession. If that obsession has left a hollow place where a soul ought to be, that is fine with him. Survival has taught him that souls are only an encumbrance. Over the years of living alone, he has developed his own compartmentalized form of relaxation. Stripped to his underwear, he sits and schizes. His blank stare and equally blank mind are only interrupted by an occasional belch. That is the essence of his life: rules, forms, furniture, schizing, and belching. Within its parameters he feels, if not content, safe.

"Sanctuary!" he screams in his wordless, broken voice, a squeal of a voice that derides his bureaucratic powers, a feedback squealed voice that screams of raging helplessness. "Sanctuary!" He believes that it is his to obtain – his right, under Heaven, under God. "Sanctuary!"

Not to be. Never to be. Not for him. Not for you. Not for me. Sanctuary? No careening truck? Dream on!

***

Orrin Partles had survived the Greek Civil War. His parents had not. His brother and three sisters had not. His wife had not. His little girl had not. But he had. He had survived the hard times and found a way to reach America. So what if he has sold his soul to this soulless state hospital. He can live without a soul. He needs no attachments. He has survived.

The weird sound of howling patients does not at first interrupt him. Screams and cries are the daily background of the asylum. He continues his mental checklist. *I have to speak to Dr. Abrose*, he thinks. *He keeps moving the furniture in his office. That youngster doesn't appreciate proper order.*

The rage of sound from the ward grows even louder. *Where are those attendants?* Partles says to himself, his thoughts finally disrupted. *This really has to stop.* He pulls the key chain from his pocket and selects the large silver skeleton key that opens all the ward doors except, of course, the secure wards. Those wards each have their own key – seven in all, each of them part of the enormous clanking cluster in his hand.

CHAPTER TWENTY-SIX

Stan never learned to let Uncle John be. After a couple days of listening to the fury behind the closed door, he would – ever so tentatively – knock. My uncle, his father, my father's brother, would yell at him to go away; but Stan would not, could not. The moth cannot ignore the candle nor the suicide the semi.

Stan would knock. Uncle John would yell and curse. Stan would knock some more. Eventually, the ogre would come out from his lair, grab his son, and hit him while hurling invectives. It was a tossup which hurt Stan more. Once my uncle's rage had been so physically and directly expressed, once his anger had been depleted, then he would return to what passed for normal in that house.

Aunt Alice would patch Stan up and tell him that his father hadn't meant it – that his father had demons deep inside him, demons that took control over him. Stan would say he understood and that he wasn't angry or upset. Meanwhile, each episode was a small step along Stan's highway, the highway that led inevitably to his death, to the scenic turnoff in California, to the pitting of motorcycle against truck.

Orrin Partles had escaped civil war only to die at that moment in an asylum version of that same ultimate, cosmic, life versus death, flesh versus unstoppable object kind of moment.

Jack – good-old raging Jack – dreamed of a military career, one to eclipse his father's service in World War II. That had been his father's defining moment – all few minutes of it. He had landed at Normandy and been shot in the ankle. Afterwards, he could not sufficiently use his foot for military service and had been returned to America. For years he used that foot as a symbol of his importance to the world throughout a career of mediocrity; used that ankle to dominate his wife and children; used his moment of pain to rationalize his whims and fancies, his screams and outrages, his arbitrariness and rigidity.

Jack had been the most scarred of the family and the most competitive with his father. He joined the army to see what he could be. He was booted from boot camp, given a section eight after the first nighttime fire drill; Jack had been so frightened that he forgot to put on his pants. Standing in his boxers in front of a barracks of peers, Jack found out what he could be, what would be his career, what would be his success: he was a nut case, a most credible crazy.

Jack has joined in our howling; with each roar of the crowd, he becomes more aroused, more enraged, more engorged with patricidal lust. He picks up one of those chrome and green chairs; perhaps it is the one that had been removed from Marilyn's room. Clearly he has become ready to bludgeon. The question is who. The answer jangles his keys outside the ward door.

Inmates become so attuned to madness. It is something like absent dogs who, at the slightest touch of the refrigerator door, instantly appear salivating underfoot. In the middle of our ululations, we all hear the sound. We turn as one toward the door. We watch Orrin Partles open it. We watch him angrily enter, words of exasperation on his lips. We watch Jack jump towards the administrator with his chrome and green weapon at the ready. We watch Jack bring the chair down on Dr. Partles head. We watch the not-so-good doctor fall to the yellowing tile floor. We watch his blood, finding no place for absorption, add its crimson to the garish uncoordinated colors of the ward – add its formless blot to the Rorschach of madness.

We watch the particles of Partles – the skin, the bone, the brain – pattern the non-descript floor. We watch him die. We watch him die, and we howl, as animals will. We howl for the soul that he had left in Greece and for the one that we know would be removed from Jack's brain.

We howl until the staff's little party breaks up. Orrin Partles has been dead for some time.

He has been dead for years.

CHAPTER TWENTY-SEVEN

"Timmy and Marilyn in a tree, f – u – c – k – i – n – g." It is Rosie's voice that she hears. Marilyn knows this is silly. Rosie's a dog, and everyone knows that dogs don't know how to spell.

Marilyn wonders, *Maybe he's under a witch's spell. That would explain it.* Rosie has always been a strange dog. Dogs really aren't supposed to lick your bumper and tickle you between the legs.

Rosie always liked to climb into bed with her. As a child she would hear him opening the door and quietly making his way to her bed. Hushed as he might try to be, she could hear his nails on the wooden floor of her bedroom. She could feel the bed sway slightly from his weight. She could feel him pulling the pillow from between her legs. She could feel his tongue exploring her, the cold wet of his nose sniffing her.

Then, as quietly as he had come, he would leave – leave her lying in the dark stillness, leave her clutching the silken fringe of her blanket, leave her stuffing a corner of that fringe into her mouth to keep from crying out – to keep her from waking the family.

Rosie never liked to chase sticks. He had always been too busy digging. When Erik died and they had buried him under the big tree in the back yard, Rosie kept trying to dig him up. It had bothered Marilyn's parents that Rosie wanted to dig up the coffin that held what looked like Erik. It hadn't bothered Marilyn. She would have helped except that would have made her parents angry. When Rosie was digging under the tree, Marilyn's father would throw things at him or come up behind him and kick him. Rosie would run kiyiing away, but he would return and start digging again. He had always been a very determined dog.

Marilyn wondered why Rosie wanted to dig up the box that held what looked like Erik. She had often asked him, but Rosie told her that it was none of her business. "Death is something for dogs to know about; people can't understand it," he had said emphatically. Marilyn wished she were a dog so she, too, could understand death.

Celeste died. That had been what they had told her. Actually, nobody had told her. The staff members who were washing her were talking about Celeste's dying. They talked as if Marilyn couldn't hear them and as if Celeste hadn't in some strange way been Marilyn's best friend in the hospital. They had talked as if Marilyn and Celeste were things, objects. They had talked in that staff way that makes patients into things. There was no disrespect intended. There had been no existence intended. There had been none taken.

The doctors had tried to fix Celeste's foot. Celeste's foot turned over so that she walked on her ankle. Since she was never going anywhere, it didn't seem to matter much. But the doctors decided to fix her foot. That way they could say they had helped her.

The operation had been a great success. When they buried Celeste her foot was nice and straight. It was too bad that she had never been awake to appreciate her fine straight foot. It was too bad that she wasn't around to piss on the black judge chair and make the man who each day came and bothered Marilyn go away.

Sometimes Celeste talks to Marilyn through the crack in the wall. Celeste talks about Rosie; they have become lovers. Marilyn wishes that she and Celeste and Rosie could all make love with Timmy Wang. She wishes that she could go inside the wall and they would chase each other through the forest.

She and Celeste speak of these things and they are no longer things; they become people. Existence is intended. Respect is intended. They are taken.

"Rosie and Celeste in a tree, l – i – c – k – I – n – g." She knows that nobody else can hear her voice. It was the special voice that she uses when she doesn't want to have a voice. It is the voice she uses to swear at the attendants who come and push food into her mouth, and at the ones who come to wash her, and especially at the man who comes in his white coat and sits staring at her.

That voice says terrible things. Sometimes Celeste tells her she shouldn't say such things. "Oplit fambolet," she says, and Celeste cringes. "Zymp rampion," she cries, and Rosie stops his barking. "Poyrer boof," she says and all meaning is clear. All existence is real. All is intended.

Once when that voice had said its magic words, Erik climbed down from a tree. He and Rosie wrestled on the ground. Unfortunately, Erik hadn't noticed where Rosie had crapped so he was covered with dog shit when he climbed back into the tree. But that didn't matter because it all happened inside the crack opposite Marilyn's bed, and Marilyn didn't have to worry about keeping bad things from happening – not in that world – not in her private cracked world.

Marilyn worries that one day she will say the magic words in a voice that can be heard. She worries what such power, once unleashed, might do. She worries that Rosie had once explained death to her even though she cannot remember his doing so. That must have been during the night while he was sniffing and licking. She worries that she might stop death –

a world without death would be a terrifying place: a place without escape, a place without a crate.

Beware the golem of the insane. Beware life that is uncontrolled. Beware! Beware everything!

***

Marilyn is trying to remember the nursery rhyme. "Hi diddle diddle could eat no fat, and all the king's horses and all the king's men fell down the hill." She tries to drown out the noises from the hallway. They are terrifying noises.

"Take all of it. "

"All of it, Bobby, or doctor will have to give you a shot."

"Valerie, where are you hiding? It's medication time."

"I'll take care of Marilyn."

She comes in looking starched white and made of plastic. She puts one hand behind Marilyn's head to prop it forward and holds a cup to her lips. The pills cascade into Marilyn's unresisting mouth. Another cup, this with orange non-juice, and the ordeal is done. Marilyn wonders why they bother giving her medicines. She wonders why they don't just kill her quickly. She wants them to kill her quickly so she can stay forever with Celeste, with Erik, with Rosie. She is sure that then she could find Timmy Wang, and they could play bumperpool forever.

Maybe that's what the judge is for – to see if I've been good enough to kill. I'll try to be very good. I won't say any of the bad words or move. Then... She drifts off to the yellow-pill sleep.

CHAPTER TWENTY-EIGHT

"Jack be nimble, Jack be quick, Jack killed the doctor with a chair," Doris sings as she dances around the dayroom. One of the aides tries to hush her, but to no avail. The duty nurse threatens her with an injection. Doris sings on. She knows – we all know – that the staff are all feeling impotent, and nothing spurs dementia like the impotence of those who are supposed to contain it.

Charlie shuffles back and forth as if he were on roller-skates. Back and forth, back and forth – wearing his way through the yellow waxy tinge of the tile floor. Back and forth, back and forth – marking eternity as surely as the petroglyphs of ancient Indians. Back and forth, back and forth – a pendulum measuring the tedium of life, bearing witness to pointlessness, a metronome for the inane.

Doris sings. Charlie shuffles. Mitch, poor demented Mitch, now relegated to one of the geri-chairs that keeps him from getting too lost on this locked ward, rocks from side to side and then from front to back. A deranged metronome, he keeps non-time – non-time for the disintegration of the world.

Jack has gone – gone to court. Was he insane? Of course he was crazy, but was he insane? The judge decides that he can take part in his own defense. Hell, he couldn't even defend Australia, but what the heck? They try him. Was he insane? He was paranoid as hell and had wild delusions, but was he insane? The jury says, "Yes." Better a jury than a judge.

Jack is returned to the hospital, to another ward. They zap him. He babbles. They zap him some more. Was he insane? He is a vegetable, but was he insane? Did it matter? Insane or not, a zucchini is still a zucchini and a rutabaga is still a rutabaga.

And Dr. Partles – he is dead. He had been dead for years, but now his body knows it. He won't stare into space and think – not anymore. He won't belch and fart – not anymore. He won't count furniture – not anymore. "Quoth the raven, 'Nevermore!'"

Stan is dead, too. Incontrovertibly, he is dead. Jamul isn't dead. "Excuse me," he sings, "while I kiss the sky."

CHAPTER TWENTY-NINE

There is, as there always is, a bureaucratic shuffle as soon as Orrin Partles's blood has been mopped into memory. When it is done, nobody has lost a job, been demoted, or even given an administrative rebuke. Of course, nobody has asked us what happened. By the time that security had been called, the party had disappeared into file cabinets on other wards. By the time security had called the police, breath mints had been liberally applied. By the time that any administrators had been called, a cassata had been rushed from a nearby bakery and chunks taken out of it. Any residual smell was simply the sweetness that goes with coffee in a long afternoon. Nobody was to blame – nobody except Jack. Jack, soon to be zapped Jack, was responsible. Orrin Partles, M.D. was dead, and the world would not be conquered. That was enough consequence for anybody.

Nobody asked us what had happened. If they had, what would we have said? We might have talked about wolves, and howlings, and lunatic things; but none of us would have dared to talk about staff parties, and alcohol, and lack of supervision. We know better. You don't say bad things about the people who carry the keys. You don't question the judgment of the people who inject butts. You don't attack the people who control the straightjackets and the rubber rooms. You can think bad things, but you must never say them.

Besides, it wouldn't have helped Jack. Normandy had been his undoing – before he was born, even before his parents had met. A poorly aimed bullet, perhaps a ricochet; that was all it took. Finally, that little piece of lead had hit its real mark – the helpless, shuffling, paranoid mind of an inmate, a resident of nowhere, a non-being in the asylum.

Beware of semis careening down the highway. Be sure that you jump – jump clear or jump directly into their paths, but never, never, get hit by the ricochet. A dead body is better than a dead brain left to shuffle in parody – endless parody – of life.

Stan had jumped the right way. Jack Abrose, sitting behind the wheel in his mindless depression, hadn't. After years of trying to keep clear, Orrin Partles has finally met his truck; Jack has once again been ricocheted into the dung heap. Did anyone ever jump clear? I don't know. What I do know is that the caves in which we hide, the crates in which we take sanctuary: they don't keep us safe. They may keep us out of the rain, but they don't keep us safe.

CHAPTER 30

Jack Abrose never escaped from his depression. His semi having killed, he withdrew himself from life. He never escaped, but then, as his family and friends who slowly deserted him to his loneliness were quite fond of reassuring themselves, he had never tried to escape.

And the depression slowly strangled him. First, he stopped work, then he stopped all driving. Next, he refused to leave the house. He withdrew to his bedroom. He stopped reading the papers, then books. His television was given to the Salvation Army. Eventually, even his radio and his bedside clock were removed from his life.

In the end, the depression strangled him. He died one night in the aloneness of his self-created worldly crate. By then his well-stomached freight-driving body had eaten itself into emaciation. By then his eyes had turned inward and sunken into his skull. By then his shock of deep-black hair had straggled and knotted into dirty gray.

The medical examiner insisted on an autopsy, which he performed to no one's interest. He found a small but fatal bleed in Jack's brain. Nobody cared, but the paperwork was done properly – it must always be done properly.

Few attended the burial. Fewer still cared that Jack Abrose was physically gone. For most he had been gone for years.

Buford, busy filling out the paperwork of his residency, doesn't bother to return home for the funeral. He knows that the relief he feels does not need some ritualization to give it validity. He sits at his typewriter that morning; he sits and writes case notes. When the hour of burial comes, he is busily writing about Marilyn – case notes on a living corpse while he ignores the one being lowered into the earth.

That evening, looking wanly at his wife, he wonders if his father had missed him that morning. She laughs anxiously, and then observes that her father-in-law could hardly have missed in death what he had been oblivious to in life.

"And he couldn't miss in life what had been oblivious to him in death," Buford responds. He says a prayer, a brief prayer, for the dead living, and the living searching to be dead.

CHAPTER THIRTY-ONE

"Sanctuary," we scream. "Sanctuary!" We, the new hunchbacks, the new deformed, we have founded a new church, the cathedral of mental illness. Devoid of God, yet serviced by chaplains – perhaps not chaplains as much as missionaries, missionaries sent by make-believe-caring people who want no contact, caring people who do not care, caring people who donate balaclavas in the heat of summer and shorts for us to wear in winter.

"Do not release your huddled masses," they say, "but give them the leavings of our church bazaars that our consciences might sleep more easily."

"Give them the unsolds of our stores that our tax deductions may show love."

A violent death in the midst of madness. "Keep them locked in. They'll murder us in our sleep. And here are woolen mittens to wear while they are locked in their secure over-heated wards."

It is cold – unforgiving cold – the kind of cold that creeps around doors and through windows. Unwelcome, unbidden, it chills not only the body but the spirit as well. The winter rain lashes at the windows and pelts off with the crack of whips. Rivers stream from leaders eroding the gravel and overflowing the sewers. The hospital is under attack from the elements. It is as if the heavens are trying to obliterate it – us. Flush madness into the sea, and what do you have? A sea of madness, a sea in which we are adrift – as if we have ever been safe at anchor.

It is during this time of complete confinement created by the conspiracy between the particles of death, law, politics, and weather that Allan washes into our unhappy lives. Allan, the latest bit of detritus to find its way onto our island of the mad, claims to be a philosopher, a searcher after true knowledge. It had, he assured us, only been with that intent that he had been watching through the windows of various women. "Knowledge requires transparency," he opines with a deferential smirk and a knowing nod, "which means that windows are there for use in both directions."

Allan takes up a position outside Marilyn's room, a position from which he can indulge his endless obsession with watching while she lies in catatonic nothingness. It is only with great effort that the aides can remove him from his sentry's duty and close him out from her care. When she is periodically folded into a geri-chair and placed along the dirt stains of the dayroom wall, he stands by her, resting against the wall with a look of extreme satisfaction. At some point he offers to feed her, and, with no objection from the ever-silent Marilyn, Allan takes over that duty – watching, ever watching as she slowly masticates and swallows.

"I am content," Allan tells Buford Abrose. "Demosthenes searched for a natural – an honest – man, and I have found – in her most primitive – the natural woman. Marilyn is total honesty. I am content."

"But she's catatonic. What on earth is natural about that?"

"I am content," Allan repeats. "Let us talk about something else."

"Well, what brought you to the hospital?"

"The police car."

"Ahh, yes, but why?"

"Because society despises the true search for wisdom. I ask you, doctor, should it be illegal to seek knowledge?"

"That depends on how – I mean, what the person does."

"Does it? I wonder. Once the members of your profession were denied the opportunity to examine the workings of the human body. Even after death the body was unstudied. That was the law. Today, we consider such laws archaic, even ridiculous. Why should my researches be any more condemned than we now condemn those early body snatchers who made medicine live? Is it not true that hope springs infernal?"

Buford, his face twisted in quizzical confusion, scribbles a note – one to which he would never return. "Hope," he writes, "what is?"

"And what is it that you wanted to find? When you peered through those windows, what were you looking for?"

"Honesty…," Allan pauses. "And, now I've found it. I am content."

"Even though you're locked up? Even though you're confined to a mental hospital?"

"My mind is free. Nothing else matters."

They sit in horrible silence, each staring into the maw of his own thoughts.

How strange, Buford Abrose thinks, *that I should find that catatonic woman so trying, so lacking in purpose, and this madman finds her enthralling – the end of his life's search. A peeping tom and a catatonic, what a strange combination.* He looks out the window of his cramped office, observes the pigeon-shitted porch that stretches the front of the redbrick building's second floor façade. *Perhaps fate is filled with such strange combinations. My father's semi and a young man's motorcycle. A lost Greek doctor and a flying chrome chair. Like magnetic charges – inexplicable attractions. Does anything end well?*

The silence stretches on. Allan's face holds the smallest trace of that smile, at once a smile and a smirk – perhaps of contentment, possibly of condescension. *How strange,* Allan thinks, *that this man should claim to be a healer of minds and yet is so unable to touch her mind – her mind so open, so waiting for human existence.*

The silence continues – two men caught in the nothingness of the sea of madness. And the rain, which is now freezing into a patina of wonder, continues, as it has for unabated days, to crack itself against our pane and into our pains.

CHAPTER THIRTY-TWO

He knows that Alice is unhappy. It would have been difficult for him to not know. Her unhappiness leaks from her pores – no, to be more honest, it flows from them in storming streams not unlike the winter rain. And, like the rain, Alice Abrose's unabating unhappiness seems determined to wear away the foundations against which it beats.

She had never liked the thought of psychiatry. She had had her hopes, long before she met Buford, when she imagined a doctor husband, one who would please her parents and give her the life which she had been brought up to expect. She hoped that one day her husband's patients would be people of wealth, people who would invite them to fancy dinners, whom they would run into at symphonies and theaters. She imagined the world of the successful physician's wife, a world of country clubs and fancy cars, of charity dinners and European vacations. She hoped for dermatology, plastic surgery, ophthalmology – something clean, something elective, something lucrative. Now, she would gladly settle for proctology. *Successful assholes are better than plain old assholes,* she thinks as she stares out the window of their apartment.

Perhaps Buford is right. Perhaps I'd be less unhappy if I found something to do with my days. But in this town, here at the end of the world, what's worth doing? It is a town that came into existence to house the syphilitic walking dead, and little has changed even since the discovery of penicillin. It seems that half the families in town make their living at the hospital, and that the second half doesn't want anything to do with the first. *Maybe they're afraid they'll catch nuttiness. Maybe they're afraid that we'll recognize that they already have it,* Alice ruminates. From her perspective, it seems that most of the town's inhabitants are only a banana peel away from life on those yellow-tinged wards with their grated windows.

Given the type of people who make up the mass of the hospital's work staff, there are no stores or businesses in which she could have sought employment even if she had wanted to, none that she would have deemed worthwhile. She doesn't see herself in Dollar Stores. She can't imagine herself ringing groceries in one of the chain stores that sell half-spoiled produce and green-turning meat. She wants no part of insurance brokers who mostly handle assigned-risk drivers with multiple tickets and frequent accidents. She has no interest in waiting on Formica tables where patients on day release drink their endless cups of coffee and try to make believe that they have somewhere to go.

This is Purgatory! Alice has already decided that. What she fears is that the future will become Hell. She imagines a lifetime of living in such mold-tainted places with a husband who will grow increasingly moody as his career deteriorates into one long prescription for phenothiazines and anti-depressants.

Every day Buford comes back to find her more angry, more withdrawn, more unhappy. And every day Buford comes back himself feeling less meaningful, more unable to do anything to help anyone.

The worst thing is her ubiquitous awareness that she has never loved him. She had gone to college to find a good life, to find the husband of her family's expectations. There had been law students, business students, and medical students: these were the ones she considered for her future. And, of all these possibilities, she picked Buford Abrose. Why? Because he had seemed so easy. No family ties with which she'd have to compete. No big ego that she would have to cut to size. *God, was I a fool*, Alice thinks as she stares out the window and contemplates the endless cold rain, the endless winter that has become her life.

CHAPTER THIRTY-THREE

My memories go back, way back – as if they reach to the beginning of time. Yet I have no memories of being toilet trained. That had been a primordial event, an archetypical knowledge passed from cave-dweller to cave-dweller, and somehow finding its re-expression in my parents' expectations.

To say that my mother was preoccupied with defecation would hardly convey her world. Cleanliness was not next to godliness, it was godliness. From her atheistic Jewish background she had assimilated only the concept of kosher. But, for her, kosher was uniquely defined to meet her ever-changing needs and perceptions. What she wanted was kosher; what she disliked was traife. Lobster was kosher; hot dogs were traife. Visiting her parents was kosher; visiting my paternal grandparents was traife. Non-Jewish friends in our house were traife. Jewish friends in our house were traife, too, but only pseudo-traife – a new category added to Leviticus.

Feces were also kosher or traife. That depended on their function as runes, runes which she read with brilliance beyond the rest of the family's ken. In parts of Germany and Holland there are toilets that have a shelf built in so that the stools can be better examined. When flushed, a sheet of water flows over the shelf and then carries the waiting feces off the shelf into the swirl that awaits. Sadly, my mother didn't have such a modern convenience. Nevertheless, each stool was carefully studied. Size, shape, number, color, subtleties of composition: all were deliberated. The result of this emphasis was constipation, and then straight-out terror – terror of her diagnoses and prognostications; more terror – much more terror – of the enemas and laxatives that were to be imposed. Life became a battle, a battle over control: control of my sphincters, control of my bowels, and from that salient, control over my movements and, indeed, over my every moment.

My stools grew in size and density. Plungers failed. Plumbers came and went. Water overflowed onto floors, over the bathroom tiles, under the door, along the hallway, down the stairs.

My father seethed, roared, and threatened. My mother cried, moaned, and begged. The laxatives and enemas lead to raging conflict within my intestines and then to – horrible moments – loss of continence: stinking, soaking, moments of school embarrassment. Teasing was inevitable. Ostracism followed. The battle continued.

Strangely, there was power to be obtained. I had first call on the bathroom. The toilet had become my throne, a throne from which to rule my own mad world.

Yet, there was ever a catch. Woe betides me if I flushed without her inspection. Having emanated from her womb, all that I was was hers, and all that emanated from me was also hers. There was no stool hiding in my world, nor could I hide the absence of stools. It was the primacy of the privy without privacy. Existential angst may be the result of our being born and dying in an ultimate state of aloneness. But the inability to be alone in the toilet also produces a different angst – or should I have dared to fart and ask her, "Whose body is it anyway?"

No wonder I seek the privacy of the bathrooms, those wonderfully stinking bathrooms, those bathrooms that made the ward seem human, those bathrooms in which I am truly allowed to be alone if only by the aversion of others.

What do I do while sitting there for as long as I dare before an aide must come to find me, to count me, to account for me, to control me with the inevitable needle of sleep, the universal solution no matter what the problem or even in the absence of a problem?

I would love to sit on the toilet and read, but I don't read. To read in the asylum is to appear sane. To appear sane is to be crazy. To be crazy is to be given a shot. A new form of Unitarian utilitarianism.

No, I don't read. I do something far more seditious. I think. I think about the nature of the world. I think about the nature of the universe. I think about God. Is He, too, taking a shit? Are we, all of us as one, in fact, the remnants of a previous divine dump? Are our lives, indeed our world, circling the bowl on our way to the wasteland of oblivion? Have we been flushed and just don't yet know our fate? Is some celestial cesspool the definitive semi? Ultimately, does it matter? Surely, we – I – won't matter. Sitting on that cracked seat resting on its equally disfigured porcelain base with one foot braced against the unlockable green door with its absurd graffiti of gas passed and lives hated – surely I don't matter – not to God, not to man, not even to myself.

CHAPTER THIRTY-FOUR

His name is Micahel, a strange name for a stranger man. Even in this disordered world, this brawny man of jerking motion, stuttered speech, and dogmatic truths seems eccentric. Through the native drums we learn that Micahels' family has been recently gathered up and then scattered through the world of mental health. He, now flotsam in our sea, has gone from pater familias to inmate familiar. Even now, wandering dazed up and down the corridors and back and forth across the day room in that new-patient haze of incomprehension, he cannot grasp the reasons for his fall.

We, on the other hand, comprehend and laugh. It is too obscene to do otherwise. It is too shitty to go unremarked.

"Shit?"

"Exactly." Arthur pauses to deliberately scratch his ass. He continues, "Shit everywhere. The whole house."

"Why didn't they use the toilet?"

"They did. They used it and used it until the cesspool was filled, until it started backing up. Then they filled the toilet. After that the bathtub, or at least I suppose it was that order. Then the sinks, bathroom and kitchen. Then the plastic bags. Piled in rooms. Plastic bags with those metal ties. Filled and piled. A dung heap beyond any imagination."

"And no one noticed?"

"Eventually. Eventually a teacher or someone. The smell must have clung. The stench, the stink of those people."

He is grinning in perverted delight. So am I. So are the rest of our little knot. We shuffle up and down the dayroom, struggling to appear disconnected, careful to stay out of Micahel's earshot, more careful to avoid the aides. Still, we cannot resist the chortles. Do denizens of Purgatory laugh at the tormented of Hell? The crazy cannot resist the comedy of the mad.

"I wonder who called."

"Probably a school nurse …"

"Or a social worker. They can never resist." We nod in understanding. Who among us has not had a social worker intrude into our life? All well-meaning, of course. Well-meaning, and endlessly destructive. More destructive than a house full of feces? Who knows? That question we defer unasked to Micahel.

He is shuffling ever faster. Does he know that we are laughing at him? He grows increasingly agitated. We watch, knowing. The aides, the valium, the rubber room await. He does not know. He cannot see that the trestle is out, that the train will hurtle into the giant hole.

He had not seen that his house would also end in a giant hole – back-hoed on one side and pushed by bulldozers from the other. It was a public health hazard. Worse, it was a public relations nightmare. What authority wanted the media, masks over faces, reporting from the stench-filled site? A quick operation at dawn and the dozers spreading lime and sandy soil over the remains. It is usually best to dispose of shit quickly. Flush and be done.

Micahel's family have also been disposed of – buried and flushed. The pieces, social detritus, have been spread like so much manure over the mental health garden. He is our piece. Everyone hold your nose and admire the stench.

***

Bill has his issues with shit, too. However, for Bill it is cat shit. More specifically it is the shit that the cat leaves in his slippers. The cat is not an inmate. She is not a member of the staff. She is a cat, a crippled, brain-injured cat brought onto the ward by Arthur at the end of a day pass, in a moment of crazed humanness.

Arthur feels lonely so he stops at a pet store. Many of us do that, stop for a few minutes to enjoy the guileless sweetness of creatures who know no better. It is easy to laugh at the tug-o-war between two pugs or the wrestling of a golden and a beagle. It is easy to feel kinship with a cockerpoo, or even to empathize with the macaw marching back and forth on his dowel perch.

He doesn't go in meaning to buy an animal. He knows that pets are not allowed on the ward. Besides which, he has no money. That is probably the biggest obstacle, at least until he saw this tiny animal staggering about in a cage. "Free," the sign reads. What inmate can resist that word?

One of the orange front paws is bent, drool leaks from her kitten mouth, she incessantly meowls in the voice of misery, and she wobbles with every movement. The humanitarian in Arthur demands the pathetic animal's rescue. "Is he really free?" Arthur asks, not believing his good luck.

"That's what the sign says."

"But why?"

"Are you kidding? Who'd buy her? I said I'd take the litter. The rest are gone, sold them all. This one I'll have to kill, that is unless ..."

"Unless I take her," Arthur finishes the thought with relish.

"Unless you take her," the store owner agrees.

So Arthur does. He smuggles the animal inside his shirt. And, with the cunning of the mad, he enters the ward talking loudly to himself so that no staff will hear the kitten's plaint.

If the staff had known, the cat would have been thrown out – to where, who knows? But nobody asks, so nobody tells. Enticed by hospital food – foolish animal – she takes up residence under Bill's bed. Arthur doesn't ask. It's a corner bed, and that seems a good idea – safer, more cave-like, and more hidden from staff view.

An old cardboard box filled with torn up paper and sand for litter. All fine – except the cat will have no part of that box. Bill has comfortable slippers, perhaps a gift from a family member with nothing less to do, still better than the hospital issue paper-thin shuffle-alongs.

Her first night under his bed the cat gives Bill a gift, left in his right slipper, loose, slightly green, and reeking. Worse, in the wee hours Bill has the need. Without looking – for who would look? – he swings his feet to the floor and feels for those slippers. Still without looking, he pushes his toes into their comfortable resting places. Then, he screams. It is a scream of loathing and disgust. It is a scream of leprosy and scrofula. It is a scream of tortured souls and broken bodies. It is the scream of one who had just stepped into a slipper filled with cat diarrhea.

We, all who share this room, are at once awake. No one speaks. Bill's horror has suppressed us. Finally, Micahel voices a hoarse demand, "What the fuck?"

It gives us permission.

"Bill, what happened?" someone hisses.

"Quiet, the aides will hear." That ubiquitous concern.

"Shit," Bill still outraged.

"What is it, Bill?"

"I told ya ... shit. His voice is a whispered scream. "That cat crapped in my slipper." He picks up the offending footwear. "Where's that fucking animal?" he insists, no longer concerned with aides or regulations. "That God-damned animal has crapped in my slipper. Fuck, fuck, fuck!" He kneels next to the bed and reaches for the cat.

It might have been comical, him kneeling there with his butt hanging out, one slipper on and the other foot covered in cat diarrhea. It might have been comical, but nobody laughs. Only Arthur speaks, "Leave my cat alone. She didn't mean ..."

"Ass hole." Bill's bass booms in the empty room.

There is a round of ssshing sounds.

"I mean it. I'll kill you." Arthur's voice trembles in prophetic rage. "I've done it before."

"What have you done?" The aide's voice takes us by surprise. The sudden switch of the lights blinds us into confusion.

"That fuck is threatening to kill me." Bill's voice rises in anger. It might be reasonable anger, but the system doesn't care.

The aide shouts. In moments there are others and a nurse wielding her needle.

Bill is felled first. He has no chance to mention the cat hidden under his bed. He has no chance to mention the diarrhea that covers his foot.

The nurse goes for another needle, and Arthur, too, is soon lying helpless on the floor. Both men are trussed and carried out.

"The rest of you be quiet or you'll get the same thing." We mumble assent and roll over as if we would somehow immediately drop away. They leave dragging the two men. We wait a moment in case one of the aides is sneaking back to catch us, to justify more shots, more straightjackets, more rubber rooms. Then the whispering. Then the quiet laughter.

Micahel offers a solution. It is simple. It is pure. It is cruel. "Kill the cat."

Arthur isn't there to object. Most of us are apathetic. The fact is that only Micahel cares one way or the other. If he hadn't suggested a solution, no one would have thought there was a problem. What's a little cat shit? What's a brain-damaged cat? What's a slipper or a couple of guys in the rubber room? Go back to sleep. Meds make you tired.

Micahel is insistent. "We have to kill it." Nobody objects. Nobody agrees. He won't let it go.

***

Some stories are too crazy even for the loony bin. Micahel's story is one of those. His parents had worked for a medium sized circus, one that toured places like Eugene and Des Moines, not the big cities, the cities of the hinterland. They had taken care of the big cats, the lions and tigers. And, oh, my, how they loved those cats. When big top economics ended their jobs and when they had a young Micahel to raise, they found a small home in the country where they could have cats, not big ones but the family pet kind. Not one cat or two or even a few, they just kept taking them in and letting them reproduce until the house, the adjacent garage, and the surrounding lot were overflowing. Inevitably there came times when the neighbors, even though they were distant neighbors, complained and threatened.

The solution? "Drown the cats." It was his father's command and Micahel's job.

Using large burlap sacks, the sacks in which they purchased bulk dry cat food and which they had stored in that falling-down, off-orange barn, and rocks gathered from the river to which they would be returned, Micahel, then a boy, would gather the cats up indiscriminately, stuff them and the rocks into those burlap sacks, and plunge them into the river. Over and over he would do so. Bag after writhing bag. Until they were all gone, all drowned. Then he would sit on the mossy, rocky bank and watch to make sure that the bags did not somehow escape, that the dead felines did not somehow come back to meowing life,

Micahel would sit watching late into the night. When he could say that he was sure, when he could tell his father that the cats were truly gone, he would trudge the half mile back to the house and go to bed. The next morning he would come down to breakfast, but his father would not ask. It was as if the cats had never existed. By evening, the next inevitable generation had been started.

How many times Micahel, the boy, the adolescent, the young man, had performed this deadly task he cannot or will not tell us. With hoarse-whispered intensity he tells us only that the cat had to be killed, that his father had commanded: "Drown the cats."

***

We, Micahel and I, slip out the metal grate that is designed to keep us locked within. A bent coat hanger key is all it takes. Perhaps the more secure wards have better locks, more secure screens. We can come and go with relative ease.

Micahel holds the cat. Surprisingly, his grip is gentle and reassuring. She seems to relax, far more so than when Arthur had held her, far more so than when she had crouched in the corner at the back of the space below Bill's bed.

I carry a ripped pillowcase. Jack had salvaged it from the linen room. You never know when you'll need something to carry stuff with, you never know what you'll need to carry, and you'll certainly never know when you'll need to drown a cat.

The fire escape is a series of metal balconies and stairways – easily descended and just as easily climbed. Careful of any passing staff, the two of us walk the two staircases to the ground. Checking for the night security staff, old men who cruise the grounds in Plymouths and try to look as if they have authority, we head for the beach.

Had the state not built this mental health fort, the grounds would have long ago been developed into high-priced housing. Perched as it is on a cliff above the sound, ironically this is a place of both sadness and beauty.

There is a long set of stairs going down to the beach, the beach which is forbidden to us and to which we often go – not to swim or sunbathe but to smoke, sometimes drink, fuck, and otherwise act as we are not supposed to. That night Micahel and I are on an equally primitive and forbidden mission, a mission of killing.

We are not alone on the beach. That doesn't matter. Nobody will interfere – a rule among inmates.

We gather small stones along the beach, slip them and the small animal into the pillowcase, tie double knots at the top and at the rip. With a twirling motion Micahel builds the bundle's momentum and then releases it in a long arc that culminates in a splash.

I know that the act is sad, but I do not feel sadness. It occurs to me that it has been cruel and wrong, but I do not feel guilt. I feel nothing, and that absence of feeling makes me uneasy. "Let's go," I hiss.

"No." He sits down on the sand and looks out on the slightly waving water.

"What?"

In a small voice, "We have to watch."

"Why? I want to get back before anyone notices."

"No, we have to watch."

"Why?" I ask again.

"In case she gets out."

"Even if she does, what difference will it make?" I am getting more uncomfortable.

"We have to!" It is the logic of the mad imperative. I sit down next to him. We wait and we watch.

I pick up a stick and start to doodle in the sand. Absently I brush the sand and erase my mark upon the world. *Is that me,* I wonder, *here for the moment and then erased – a mark in the sand of time?*

CHAPTER THIRTY-FIVE

"Hello, Marilyn." He has decided to try to make her more aware of his presence. "It's Dr. Abrose."

She makes no sound or motion of recognition. But inside, within her head, she recognizes him. Inside she hopes, as she has hoped before, that one of the serpent penises of Timmy Wang, one of the winding, slithering, sliming, big-mouthed penises will reach out and devour this intruder as he walks past the crack in the wall.

Once again Timmy fails her. Buford sits down in his judge's seat. She watches him from the corner of her eye, ever wary of what he might do to her. She imagines him disintegrating into atoms, but when she glances again from the corner of her eye, he is still sitting there. *Bastard*, she thinks. *Cock sucking bastard. Eat shit and die. Die and eat shit.*

Buford sits looking at his patient and dealing with his frustration. Even inept Corrie Snyder has made some contact with her catatonic patient. Only Buford is getting nowhere. Not that the patient's farting when Corrie comes into the room is a major recognition. But at least it affirms her existence.

Damn you, Marilyn, he thinks. *I don't need this. What the hell am I gonna present at grand rounds? 'She lies staring at the wall?' I've written 'no change' until my hand is ready to fall off?*

He imagines his hand falling to the floor holding the gold pen his wife had given him, back when she had more hope, when he graduated from medical school – the pen which is now so carefully tucked away beneath his underwear, where it awaits, as does he, as does his wife, a future of paying patients and a meaningful life. In his imagination the hand is still alive, moving about the room on the tips of its fingers with the pen held firmly between its thumb and forefinger like a golden phallus. He imagines it climbing up the side of the bed, pulling itself from finger-hold to finger-hold like a mountain climber making his way to the top of K-2.

The hallucination holds him mesmerized. He wonders what it is that he unconsciously wants that imaginary hand to do. It reaches the pillow and climbs up her ear. Making its way down the slope of Marilyn's forehead and across her eyebrow, it reaches the bridge of her nose. Precariously, it sets about writing. Buford is reminded of the Book of Daniel. What immutable truth is about to be revealed?

Marilyn is unaware of the hand perched on her nose. She is, however, very aware of Celeste. Celeste is defecating under the tree where Erik and

Rosie didn't play fetch. As the turds drop from her crouched body, they take life and run toward Marilyn. It seems at any moment they might break through the boundaries and swarm like bees about the room.

Will they smother her? Will they turn and attack the judge in his white coat sitting in his judge chair? She doesn't know. It doesn't seem to matter. Celeste is singing, or perhaps it is someone imitating Celeste. "Time goes by so slowly; yet, time can do so much. I need your turds, I heed your turds, God speed your turds to me. Lonely urine flows to the sea, to the open arms of the sea."

Another voice interrupts. "The itsy bitsy spider climbed up the water spout; down came the rain and washed the spider out; out came the sun and dried up all the rain, and the itsy bitsy spider drowned anyway."

The hand has completed the first word on Marilyn's unmoving nose. Buford shifts his body just enough to make it out. The hand has written DEATH and is slowly making room before the next word.

Do I wish her dead? Buford asks himself. *I'm irritated, but I'm not enraged. At least I don't think I'm that angry.* The hand is still carefully writing in neat block letters.

As small a movement as Buford has made, Marilyn is suddenly and terrifiedly aware of it. She is watching him so warily that she almost misses the dance. The turds are doing a Can-Can, tossing themselves into the air as if they are rhythmically lifting their legs. The dance disintegrates into a diarrheic chaos. Marilyn begs Celeste to take control, to stop the careening turds before they fill the crack in the wall opposite her bed, before they cut her off from the world of her mind. Celeste doesn't listen. She just keeps crapping.

The turds turn into fetuses wrapped in their placentas. Marilyn tries to keep track of their sexes. *Boy, boy, girl, girl, girl, boy, girl,* she counts, but she knows that there is no way to keep track. *Which ones have I counted?* she asks herself as if it mattered.

Meanwhile, the turd-fetus chaos continues. *It's the beginning-end of the universe, a big bang boom,* Marilyn thinks. *God is coming, and She's really pissed. Will She piss on me? How will I know? Will I drown in God's urine?*

The hand has completed its second word: IS. *Death is,* thinks Dr. Buford Abrose as he watches his hand, severed from his body, writing a holy message on the nose of a catatonic schizophrenic patient with whom he has spent so many hours, during which she has urinated twice and never even farted. *Death is what?* he wonders, watching with fascination as the disembodied hand writes on.

Turds and fetuses, thinks Marilyn, watching the chaos of her schizophrenia dance beyond the crack in the wall opposite her bed. *Turds and fetuses and urine and Celeste.* She feels overwhelmed. She wants to shut out the chaos that is threatening to overwhelm her. She dares not close her eyes with the judge sitting in the room. She fixes her gaze on one fetus. *That's me*, she thinks. The fetus that is her falls off a pile of turds and lands so that she is on her head. She sees that the fetus that is her has a penis. *That's good*, she thinks when an unraveled coat hanger reaches through the crack and pokes its end through the fetal eye and out the back of its head. *It's nice that I had a penis even if I was an abortion.*

LONG writes the hand. A freckle on Marilyn's nose makes it hard for Buford to tell if the G is really perhaps an O, but that wouldn't have made sense anyway. *Death is long*, Buford Abrose reads to himself. *That's certainly true.* But the hand hasn't finished writing.

His fascination grows with each letter. His eyes are riveted to Marilyn's nose. Careful not to lose its perch, the hand writes on. E. He is reading each letter. N, O, U, G, H. With the final H, the hand slides off Marilyn's face, down the side of the sheets, drops to the floor and scurries over to Buford's leg. It pulls on his pant leg to get his attention. He reaches his arm down, and the hand reattaches itself.

Taking a clean page from his notepad, Buford, using a BIC pen, copies the words from Marilyn's nose. This will be his contribution to the next Grand Rounds. *Death is long enough.*

He slips the pen back into his shirt pocket, making sure that the clip is firmly in place. *I wonder if there's something cheaper than a BIC?* he thinks to himself as he looks at his watch.

"I see our time is up for today, Marilyn." He rises from the black chair and crosses the room, blocking for a moment Marilyn's view of the world behind the crack. When he has passed her line of vision, the scene has changed. Erik is throwing a stick for Rosie to not fetch. Rosie is jumping excitedly.

The turd is leaving, Marilyn thinks. *The turd is leaving. All's right with the world.*

***

Buford leaves the door ajar as he exits Marilyn's room. From the hallway she can hear someone singing to himself. "I once was blind, but now I see; was bound, but now I'm free." It is Allan – Allan who has waited patiently for Buford to leave Marilyn again in his charge. "Was bound, but now I'm free."

Later, after Buford has left the room, after he has left the ward, he sits in his little office wondering if life is also long enough. Then, when he can not see it, when he can not appreciate it, then Marilyn has one of her moments of agitation. Her body convulses wildly. Her eyes roll. Spit dribbles from her mouth. The spit foams with words. "Cock sucker, cunt, ass wipe, douche bag, piece of shit, crap hole." On and on the words flow. Then they are done. She is done. She has reentered her silent, unmoving world. But it is too late. The aide is already coming. The Valium is in the nurse's syringe. The restraints are in an aide's hands. There will be no calling them back. Once the asylum has started to move it is inexorable.

CHAPTER THIRTY-SIX

We call her Winona. We have always called her Winona. Of course, never to her face; that would have bought a day in the rubber room, a day bouncing off gray padded walls, a day with arms stretched firmly across the chest and tied behind the back, a day impersonating death. But behind her back, that is what we call her. She is an aide, Mrs. Wilson to us – at least for public use. Annette to the rest of the staff. But behind her back, she is Winona – nicknamed by Celeste, when she was still alive, when she still had a deformed ankle, when she still visited Marilyn. Winona. It had been because of her love of country music. Some would have opted for Dolly, but Celeste had insisted, "Her jugs just don't live up to Dolly." And we all had to agree.

She had arrived on the ward one sunny day, singing and doing a graceless little two-step every now and again. We had all liked her immediately, liked her enough to warrant giving her a nickname that suggested humanity. We have other nicknames for other staff, but most of them are as degrading as the staff member's attitudes are towards us. In the sure and certain faith that there is no justice in this life or the next, those names are one of our little rebellions, our little evenings of the score. Ass Wipe, Stone Silence, Forms-Aplenty: those are a few of the names we use among ourselves. Others come from the comics: Palooka, Dick Traceless, and Peanuts.

But there are some staff who make our world a better place. Their reward is minimal: an extra thank you, a smile, a friendly nickname. In the economy of asylum life, these seem far greater than they would in the real world, the world only three hundred forty-seven paces from the building's front door.

Exactly three hundred forty-seven paces – that is all the distance in the world. I've walked it many times. Most of us asylum dwellers have. On any decent day, drivers following old Route 38 can see us standing around the gate, leaning on the fancy brickwork that creates an imaginary fence – a fence that scares those drivers into sanity and reassures us that we don't have to be sane. Madness has its rewards, and they go far beyond the proverbial three hots and a cot.

My paces are two feet nine inches long. That's the same as thirty-three inches. Three hundred forty-seven paces means eleven thousand four hundred fifty-one inches, or nine hundred fifty-four and one quarter feet, or three hundred eighteen and one twelfth yards, or three hundred and forty-seven paces. It isn't a long way – not like the distance to Tipperary, which is a nowhere town in Ireland, or the distance an ECT treatment has to travel to find the crazy thoughts it's meant to extinguish. It's just far enough so that parents wanting to instill fear in helpless children and husbands wanting to instill fear in even more helpless wives can drive by that gate and point to the looming red-brick monsters waiting behind it, to the mismatched humanity gathered around it, and warn of impending doom if behavior doesn't improve, if obsequiousness isn't sufficient.

I'm sure that Ass Wipe, Stone Silence, Forms-Aplenty, Palooka, Dick Traceless, Peanuts, and all the other ignominiously nicknamed staff have people who like them, perhaps even love them, out there, beyond that gate – beyond those three hundred forty-seven paces. But there is something that happens to them when they cross that threshold that takes away their humanity and therefore forces them to try and take away ours. It is a mystery like the sublimation of iodine from solid to gas – no stopping in between. Winona is one of the few who has managed to avoid that transformation. Sunny of disposition and always polite, she makes us feel like old friends – but friends with whom she can, when necessary, be stern. She is a stickler for the rules and not one to hesitate before consigning one of us, her old friends, to the rubber room. At least she enforces the rules with warmth that makes the consignee feel that she is truly sorry that the transgression has taken place and that, therefore, the consequences have become inevitable.

If any member of the staff mourned Celeste, it had been Winona. If any staff member mourned the destruction of Charlie's mind, the slow passing of Mitch's, the psychosurgical removal of Jack's, it had been Winona. She mourns with us and she mourns for us, which endears her to us.

Winona's personal life is another matter. Married to one of the recreational therapists, whom we call Slim Jim both because of his tall, thin build and his love for those overly-seasoned rolls of rawhide, fat, and mystery meats that make his breath peel the thoughts from our heads, Winona is really in love with Mr. Dixon, one of the directors of maintenance, a man of little personality and even less warmth. We assume that he more than makes up for those deficiencies with unusual sexual prowess. One thing is certain, whenever they have disappeared into an empty office for twenty minutes or more, Winona reemerges with a wondrous smile and an even greater than usual measure of happiness. We have christened him the sex-bot and have envied them their pleasures.

After many months of cheating, Winona has finally told her husband that she wants a divorce. That had been the reason for the party that ended in Orrin Partles' death; her work friends were celebrating Winona's impending freedom. Perhaps, if they had been more positive about her choice as to what to do with that manumission, the party would have been less raucous, we would not have gone a-howling, and the collision of Jack-held chrome and Naugahyde chair and Partles' head might not have occurred. Be that as it may, none of us blamed her – not even Jack. Of course, neither he nor Dr. Partles were any longer capable of blaming anyone.

Slim Jim was not so kind in his evaluation. He blamed his unhappy wife and he blamed her lover. I guess he blamed himself, as well. Two months after they separated, at the end of a long day of work trying to get someone, anyone, to do something, anything that could be called recreation, Slim Jim went home, at least to what had become home for him, a studio apartment near the train station. He wrote a letter to his wife telling her that he still loved her and could never forgive her, took out a semiautomatic pistol that had belonged to his father, put its barrel into his mouth, pulled the trigger, and blew his brains out.

It was a measure of the importance of his job that nobody noticed his absence for a week – that is, no staff. Inmates notice everything. Finally, one of his friends, another recreation aide, went to find him. Find him he did: blood and brain matter, flies and smell, gun with one shot missing, hole in head, death on a light-blue, coffee-stained carpet.

Eventually, we were told that he had resigned for reasons of health. By that time, everyone capable of hearing knew the truth. One of the rules of working in the asylum is that you must always be ethical enough to lie.

Winona has not married the sex-bot. They have lived together for a few months. However, it turns out that he is preoccupied with having children, and that she is equally determined to avoid them. So he is already looking to go on to another woman, and she is mourning – for whom: sex-bot, Slim Jim, her sex life, her self – that is open to question. Country music no longer seems to cheer her. Her smiles have stopped. Her pleasantries have ended. As surely as Orrin Partles' life has ended, Winona's life has come apart. Through the flimsy doors of the ward we can hear her crying. Lies lead to flies; flies lead to dies; dies lead to cries. Life and death in the asylum.

CHAPTER THIRTY-SEVEN

Copulation, coupling, procreation, intercourse: sex by any other name does not smell as sweet. The thick, sweet, fish smell of screwing is a consummation greatly to be desired. Except – except!

Who is using whom? Who has volition, and who has none? If we are guided by the animal within and have not capacity to judge, to make choices, what is that? Desire driven by lust is certainly not love. Hence, it reeks of sin and degradation. The fish becomes rotten – rotten like the teeth of patients who have lived too long on carbohydrates without toothbrushes or pastes.

The asylum is an olfactory world – just ask the paranoid schizophrenics. Yet, of all those odors, of all that redolency of smells, sex stands out, stands alone. It wafts through the hallways, around the flimsy closed doors that make believe they partition the ward, into the offices, into the dayroom, into the nurses' station with its gleaming antiseptic containers of pills, pills, pills.

Pills and smells mark life on the ward. Sex – lust driven animalized degradation – is its punctuation.

Doris is the sniffer dog. At the slightest hint on the wind, her antennae seek out arousal. And, by her own intense levels of arousal, she keeps herself safe from the predators of the world around her. Many patients are not so safe. Men and women alike are sought out in the noisy silence of the night. Wakened by another body pushing its way into one's bed and then into one's body, we suffer in silence. These are beings of power – power over us. They hold the keys, the pills, the syringes. They hold the power.

Occasionally, a condom malfunctions – or perhaps goes unused – and one of the women becomes pregnant. Then the last male patient to be seen speaking with her must be blamed and an abortion performed. In a moment of lucidity, Jack once suggested to me that one reason for having coed wards was the ease with which putative fathers could be named and real ones denied.

Carol, perhaps the quietest and most pious of our denizens, is also the prettiest and the most naive. Each of her pregnancies has been met by her denial of sexual activity and her intense belief that she has been visited by the Holy Spirit. The rough-handed treatment of the medical ward only further convinces her that she has been the intermedium of Christ's suffering.

It could not have come at a worse time for what little balance remains in our sad, mad world in miniature, but Carol is once again pregnant. We have a bizarre sexual trio – the guilt-ridden and abandoned Winona singing her blues, the hellaciously provocative Doris chasing every pair of pants in her unconsummated wish for sex that is not to be, and virginal Carol carrying once more The Christ Child.

We know that John is the father. I know that I am not. Nevertheless, I am the one who is to be blamed. It is – in the administration's world fantasy – my turn. I am transferred to another more restrictive ward for a month as punishment while my theoretical child is ripped from Carol's virginal womb.

The more things change, the more the madness remains the same. I return, grateful that nobody has decided to use my body for a surgical rotation, and found that the only member of our little community who has changed in my absence is Buford Abrose. It seems as if the strain of dealing with the never changing pain of our lives has begun to take a toll on his. He looks drawn, ill at ease, nervous. And he looks more human. That is the most telling of all – he definitely looks more human.

CHAPTER THIRTY-EIGHT

Jamul is holding up his customary wall this Sunday. "Look at the sky turn a hellfire red. Somebody's house is burnin' down, down, down, down, down, down, down," he screeches.

I wonder whose it will be.

"Look over yonder," Jamul wails, "he's comin' my way. When he's around I never have a happy day."

Uncomfortable, I move away from our air-guitar troubadour. I drift – no sense in drawing attention through purposeful movement. I drift as plankton on the seas of despair.

I watch the cars dribbling onto the grounds, cars filled with afflicted unwilling visitors. I no longer have visitors. That tiny stream dried up long ago. Consumed by their own fast paced lives, they have no time to spend on the unchangability of mine. The river of life has carried them along in its current, and they have left me behind. Anchored as I am to the rock of madness, I will not be swept away. Indeed, I can only drift to and fro, fro and to in the eddy that has become my world, in the time that is Jamul's concert.

Jamul's voice rises over the sad group of us. "Well, I'm up here in this womb, I'm lookin' all around. Well, I'm looking out my belly button window, an' I see a whole lotta frowns. An' I'm wondering if they don't want me around."

CHAPTER THIRTY-NINE

We are decorating the ward for Thanksgiving. The staff sloths about with decorations which they slough here and there in planless indifference. Occasionally, somebody will stick one of those decorations into a patient's hands. Then it is carried aimlessly about until another staff member recovers it and sticks it to the wall with a, "This is a good spot, don't you think?" The patient doesn't answer. Why should we?

Why should we? The staff member isn't listening for an answer anyway. The decorations don't care; they all fall to the floor or are peeled from the walls time after time until they have all found their way into the trash.

Winona puts an orange and green turkey into my hand. In the other hand I hold my cigarette. I am busy puffing, too busy to worry about a cardboard turkey. I let it drop. Winona bends over and picks it up. "Put it on the wall," she urges. I look at her with practiced blankness. "Here," she says and gently but firmly moves me towards a spot that has not yet been bedecked. I stand facing the wall – a small child standing meekly in the corner for an unknown offense – waiting for forgiveness, for an end of embarrassment.

She takes the bird from my hand. I blow smoke against the wall. She does as the dance requires and tapes the silly thing up. She intones those requisite words: "This is a good spot, don't you think?" Well practiced in my role, I say nothing. Instead, I pull another cigarette from my shirt pocket and light it from the butt that I then grind under my foot. "You shouldn't do that," Winona complains ever so softly into my ear. I say nothing. Instead, I blow another blast of smoke against the wall. She turns away, and I stare at the turkey wondering if I am supposed to be thankful – if there is something to be thankful about.

How many Thanksgivings has it been? I long ago lost track.

***

Somebody has put another turkey made of paper and cardboard in Marilyn's room. It stands against the wall across from her bed. Looking into the crack of her world, she sees the head of the make-believe turkey.

It seems strange to Marilyn that people want to make so many make-believe things when there are so many interesting things that they could see if they were only willing.

Rosie is fascinated by the turkey. He comes over to smell it and barks a few times. Erik and Celeste are playing jacks. Celeste isn't very good at games; playing is not part of the curriculum when one is studying how to be crazy. Repeatedly the ball bounces away, and Celeste scurries after it. Each time she comes back with a different ball. They are all made of turds.

Marilyn wonders if Erik and Celeste will start to dance. Once, long ago, she had liked to dance. When her cousin Jackie had married, Marilyn spent almost the entire evening dancing about. She danced alone. She hadn't wanted to dance with anyone, not even her father. Perhaps if Timmy Wang had been there, but he hadn't.

She had danced the evening away. She danced her own steps to the rhythm she heard in her own mind.

People told her that she was very cute in her pink and white dress trying to make her body move in ways that she could only imagine. "I want to be a dancer," she told the people. They told her that she would be very good. Marilyn knew they were lying. She has never understood why people want to lie.

Lying never makes anyone feel good. Or does it? Life is so filled with lies: This won't hurt. You'll be fine. Don't worry; I'll take care of it. I know you can do it. Of course I know how to operate a simple motorboat. We don't know where Timmy Wang went. The doctors are trying to understand. You didn't do anything wrong. Everybody loves you. Erik is with God.

Only Rosie and Celeste have never lied to her. Celeste peed on the green and chrome chair. Rosie jumped up and down, and tried to dig up what looked like Erik, and refused to play fetch. Those were truths. She was glad to know there were some truths.

Do I lie? she wonders. *I lie in this bed. If I got up would I still be lying?*

One of the turd balls starts to laugh. Celeste throws it and yells, "Fetch, Rosie!" Marilyn is laughing, too, but no one can see or hear her. The turd ball has turned into a fetus. It is laughing, too. Marilyn wishes that she could have stayed a fetus.

She had had a fetus once, but the doctors lost it. She didn't understand how they did that. They told her it wasn't where it was supposed to be. She wondered where they misplaced it.

Marilyn had been very young then. She wasn't sure how the fetus got inside her. Perhaps it was from eating too much sugar. Her mother always told her sweets were bad for her. She'd been sorry to lose the fetus. One should never lose the things that belong to one. That was careless. She knew she had been careless even though she was very responsible about letting Rosie out, making sure he had food and water, and picking up the yard when he left his piles of crap. She had been careless and lost something very valuable. She had lost the fetus that had been inside her. She thinks it is too bad that she was so careless while her mother hadn't been able to lose the cancer worm. *Life is like that*, she thinks. *You lose the things you want, and you can't lose the ones you don't.*

In her mind, she had told Timmy Wang about the fetus. In her mind, he had been very excited about her having a fetus inside of her. She knew he was very excited because his penis got hard and big and looked more like a hairless pool cue than it usually did. In her mind they played bumperpool right then and there, and he told her she was his very best friend. She told him he was one of her two best friends.

"Who's the other?" he demanded.

"Rosie, silly."

"Oh."

Even though she was his best friend, he left her. Timmy Wang and Wang Po had disappeared. So Timmy hadn't been there to really tell about having the fetus inside her. He hadn't been there to tell about losing the fetus. She wonders if he would have been excited, or if he would have been angry, or maybe sad.

The judge comes into her room. He stops at the foot of her bed, blocking her view of Erik and Celeste playing jacks. *Did he ever play bumperpool?* she wonders.

***

Buford is standing by the head of the paper and cardboard turkey. "Thanksgiving is almost here," he says in a pleasant voice. She remembers the voice. It is the voice of her teacher in sixth grade. He liked to tell her silly things like "Thanksgiving is coming," and then he'd give her a kiss. He didn't kiss the other girls, but he told Marilyn that she was special.

One day he asked her to take off her dress. Marilyn always liked taking off her dresses and running around in her panties. He put his arm around her and patted her on the rear end. It had been a nice pat. Then he kissed her and taken off the bra, which her aunt had bought for her a few months earlier. He had touched her nipples, and a funny feeling ran through her like an excited scared shaking; it reminded her of feelings she had felt before, feelings she had felt when she played bumperpool with Timmy Wang.

Then her teacher had pulled down her panties and touched her bumper. He was not as careful as Timmy Wang. She could see his wong getting bigger and bigger under his pants. He reached down and unzipped his pants. He pulled out his penis and picked Marilyn up, setting her on his desk. She was surprised that he knew how to play bumperpool. He moaned a lot while they were playing. She wondered if she had hurt him. When he finished, she said, "I hope I didn't hurt you."

He laughed and zipped his pants; he told her to get dressed. He kept his back turned to her while she put on her panties.

She had trouble fastening her bra. "Could you help me?" she whispered. He didn't turn around so she stuffed the bra into her book bag.

Then she put on her dress.

"This will be our secret," he said. She already knew it wasn't a good idea to talk about bumperpool so she didn't even tell Timmy Wang.

The only one she told had been Rosie. He said, "Arf" and jumped up and down. She threw a stick for him to not fetch.

Buford Abrose continues to his black chair and sits down. *Does she know what Thanksgiving is?* he asks himself. He wonders what Marilyn might have to give thanks about. When the aide comes to feed her Thursday, he will bring a special plate. The hospital administration always tries to have special holiday meals. There will be turkey, stuffing, greenbeens, and mashed potatoes. There will be cranberry sauce and apple pie. The food will be overcooked and tasteless. Only the cranberry sauce will taste the way it should; that comes from a can. Buford wonders if Marilyn will actually eat any of it or just let it dribble out of the corners of her mouth.

His thoughts turn to his own life. He wonders what his Thanksgiving will be like. His wife's family is coming. There will be the usual chitchat, the usual formal minuet of a family dance. Then, some time between the oohing over the turkey and the clearing of the table for dessert, there will come the pregnant – or, more honestly, the non-pregnant pause. With her requisite clearing of the throat, his mother-in-law will ask if they have given any more thought to children. "Now while you're both young and healthy. Now's the time. Why Norma... I don't mean to compare, but your cousin Norma is pregnant again."

Once again they will not have the heart to dash her hopes. Perhaps someday they'll adopt. Maybe they'll use a surrogate. Maybe they will just divorce. It is hard to say. Buford will look at his wife and see the anger and disappointment in her eyes. "Let me help you with the clearing," he'll say, wanting to escape, wanting to be anywhere but in that conversation. They will hear the hushed conversation through the swinging door between the dining room and the kitchen.

When they come out carrying the crystal bowl of trifle and the dessert dishes, there will be a guilty clearing of throats. "What about those Red Wings?" his father-in-law will ask, as if he or anyone at the table cares.

Am I thankful? Buford wonders. *For?* He takes the gold pen from his shirt pocket. his graduation present. He has brought it out of retirement. He no longer sees a reason to keep it for private patients. He has stopped believing that there will ever be a lucrative practice in the city. He has stopped thinking of himself as a healer. He has become, as the system has demanded, a pusher of pills into the unwilling mouths of the hapless. That is what he has become; that is what he will be. The pen has lost its promise; his life has lost its promise. He might as well; it might as well. There is no purpose.

Buford turns to a new page of lined paper. After sitting for ten minutes unable to write anything, he turns to Marilyn. "Are you afraid of dying?" he asks.

Marilyn listens to the roaring sound of his words. It was as if he is whirling an aboriginal instrument for capturing the sounds of the universe. *Rosie's dead*, she thinks.

Am I? he reflects.

Not knowing what else to do or say, he says, "Our time is up for today."

Poor Rosie, Marilyn thinks. *Poor, dead Rosie.*

Sometimes she seems better, he says to himself.

Maybe he's better off, Marilyn tells herself.

Morbid thoughts on the holidays, Buford Abrose supposes to himself. *What holidays do to us!* He pushes himself up, looks down on Marilyn's expressionless face, and says, "Have a good holiday."

How idiotic, he thinks as he leaves the room. *I might as well have been talking to that crack in the wall.*

CHAPTER FORTY

It's hard – so hard – to survive that eternity which is life without purpose. What might Stan's purpose have been if he had allowed himself to dare, to defy, to become? Would he have mastered the jazz that is life, music with multiple rhythms, music with those powerful solos that rip at the heart? Or, would he have burned out, unable to dance the macabre dance in which we blend our inner animal with the challenge of civilization? As a lover of life, would he have fallen prey to the hypnotizing beauty of destruction? Would his music have risen in crescendos of screeching horror, or would it have found itself – found him – in a voice that would reach the soul?

What ifs are so tempting. The possibilities of the unlived stretch in so many directions. There have been times – times when my own lack of meaning has forced me to the brink – that I have lived vicariously – not through Stan's life as it was, but through my fantasies of what it might have been.

Or perhaps Stan's concrete ending was its purpose. From the unrelenting hardness of his father's rage to the unrelenting hardness of the highway – did my cousin need to find the hardest knocks? What if he had survived that truck, that road? Would he have had to find another? Might he have found a life of pain following pain, agony after agony? The masochist may enjoy his pain, but does he, in the long list of his sufferings, ultimately prefer its end?

***

If jazz is the music of life, how can we describe the music of the asylum? Discordant, raucous, lacking in form, it is the music of a creeping, groaning machine. The sound does not uplift, nor does it invite introspection. Its emotions are anxiety and loss. It is not sad, because it does not care. Wheels squeal in resistance to one another; off-key notes of electric energy fill the air like errant bolts of lightening from a demented god. Bangs and crashes of doors and tempers provide erratic tympani. One cannot dance in the asylum. However much one may whirl about the dayroom, it is not dancing. Dancing requires freedom. Music, real music, requires freedom.

At Christmas there is a party put together by the recreation department. We are served overly sweet cookies, cupcakes, and fruit punch. We are given presents gathered by well-meaning congregants of local churches – gifts of little use except to the consciences of the givers. Then there is the entertainment – the expression of our own talents. Invariably there is a dance of paretics – a syphilitic shuffle done by old men whose brains have long been eaten away by their untreated sexual desires. They lurch from side to side – each out of time with his own music.

Jamul plays his air-guitar and sings, "Well, she's walkin' through the clouds with a circus mind that's running wild. Butterflies and zebras and moonbeams and fairytales. That's all she ever thinks about. Riding with the wind." He wails and wha-whas. We stare and wait for more food. Will it be candy or popcorn? That is the question of moment. Once that batch of carbohydrates for our pudgy bodies is gone, the staff tries to lead some carols. Some of us sing. We don't remember the words. We are as discordant, as off-key as the world in which we live. The night is not silent. Our nights are never silent. They are never holy. They are haunted.

CHAPTER FORTY-ONE

It has been a special bumperpool day. All the patients are in the dingy off-yellow day room. There are nonsectarian holiday decorations hanging on almost every wall in the ward. Even the crack in Marilyn's room has a festive garland of green plastic draped across it.

Marilyn sits locked in her chair and staring at the feigned festivities around her.

The nurses and aides are wearing holiday hats and roaming around wishing the patients "happy holidays." There is a pile of gaily-wrapped packages stacked in one corner of the room. Donated by a local church, they came marked M, F, or E so they could be given to someone of the appropriate sex. Over those letters the staff have hurriedly pasted holiday labels with pictures of Santa Claus and the names of patients.

"Let's see what Santa brought for Mrs. Rosenbloom," one of the nurses says. Esther, the manic depressive whose room is across from Marilyn's, claws the package open and spews it, contents and wrappings alike, onto the grimy floor. It had once been a child's Girl Scout project; now it is a scatering of beads, littering the floor, waiting to be swept up and thrown away. It had been manic Mrs. Rosenbloom's present – a beaded handbag not fit for holding, the perfect gift for the mad. It has met its ultimate use, reached its ultimate end.

One of the aides brings a package to Marilyn. "Shall we open this, Marilyn?" Receiving no response, the aide comments, "Isn't it beautifully wrapped?" She tears open the wrapping. It is a pink woolen ski hat. "Oh, this will look lovely on you when you go out," the aide says. Somehow, she seems to believe in the power of Christmas to heal the schizophrenic. She slips the hat onto Marilyn's head and walks away. Perhaps she believes that in this overheated humid dayroom Marilyn will decide to go skiing. Perhaps she believes that parboiling Marilyn's brain will cure her. Most likely, she simply doesn't care.

Another aide comes around with cookies and drinks – carbohydrates, always more carbohydrates. He feeds Marilyn half a cookie and washes it down with a few sips of watered-down eggnog. "Merry Christmas," he exclaims to the air. He starts to walk away and turns back. "Your new hat is the same color as your slippers." A fashion statement has been made.

A chorus from the church comes in from another ward. They sing some carols and go around shaking patients' hands and wishing them well. A few take Marilyn's unresisting hand and shake it. Marilyn stares straight ahead.

I wonder where Timmy Wang is today. It seems like forever before they roll Marilyn chair back to her room and help her, first to the bathroom to change her and then into bed.

Next to Marilyn's bed is another wrapped package. One of the aides picks it up and reads the label. "To Marilyn From Dr. Abrose," she reads.

"Isn't that nice, Marilyn? Doctor Abrose has left you a present. Shall I open it for you?" She rips off the paper and opens the box. Inside is a new pair of green slippers. "What a lovely present," the aide exudes. She puts them next to Marilyn's bed and picks up the old pink ones to recycle through the clothing room.

The aide leaves Marilyn propped in bed, the pink ski hat still on her head.

There is a red-brown mixture dripping from the plastic garland that someone had strung across the wall opposite Marilyn's bed. "What is that?" Marilyn asks.

"My present to you," answers Celeste. She has a large box of candy, which she is stuffing, box, wrapper, and all, into her mouth.

"Thanks, but I didn't get you anything."

"It's hard to get people presents when you're catatonic."

"Do you think I should stop?"

"That's up to Rosie."

"I never knew that," Marilyn muses. "Rosie," she calls. She keeps calling, "Rosie, Rosie" Her voice becomes louder and more anxious.

"Where is he?" she asks Celeste with exasperation.

"Hiding from you."

"Why?"

"To keep from answering."

Erik comes over to Celeste. He is crawling on all fours. He is naked, and Marilyn notices that he is now growing hair under his arms and around his genitals. "What do you think?" Marilyn asks him.

In answer Erik reaches his head between his legs and licks his scrotum. "Bad boy," screams Rosie running over and biting him on the butt. "God won't love you if you do that."

Erik looks ashamed, but he keeps licking. As he licks, his pubic hair grows longer and curlier. "It's black," Marilyn observes.

Rosie growls at her. "You shouldn't have, you know."

"Shouldn't have what?"

"Made me shit outside."

"Is that why I'm catatonic?"

"Of course not. I just wanted to use the rugs." He climbs on top of Erik's back and drags his ass along it. When he has climbed off, Marilyn can see a clear line of dog shit running the length of Erik's back. "Fuck you," says Rosie, and he runs away.

"But I still don't know," pleads Marilyn after him.

"I made it for you," interjects Celeste. "Your present, I made it for you. I shoved candy canes up my bum and shat out that lovely decoration just for you."

"I appreciate that Celeste. It's much nicer than your pee."

"I hope you like the slippers," Buford suddenly comments from outside of her world. "I thought it was time for you to have a new pair." He tries to think of something else to say. Inanely, he adds, "They go well with your new ski hat."

He has slipped in when she wasn't looking. Now, he stands beside her bed looking down at her. "I'm on call," he explains to her as if she wants to know, as if she can understand. "I had to come in anyway so I thought I'd come by and wish you, you know, a Merry Christmas."

Perhaps it is habit or just a weariness that comes over him, but he crosses the room and settles into the chair. "Personally, I've always hated the holidays," he confesses. "Do you like them? I mean, did you before – before you got sick?" He waits for the answer he knows will not come.

"When I was a kid, my parents didn't have a lot of money. What we did have my mother always wanted to give to poor people. I guess she didn't know we were poor, too. Mostly I got the joy of giving. I like that feeling. Maybe I should have become a minister. I wanted to, you know. Did you know that? I guess not."

Marilyn can smell the alcohol on his breath. It has a strange, festive quality to it. She almost wants to say something in response. *Perhaps he can tell me,* she thinks. *Perhaps he knows.* Buford is squirming uncomfortably in the black chair.

"You know, I really don't like this chair. I wish I had never asked them to change it. This one's worse than that green one. It makes me feel so…," he pauses searching for the word. "… so official, like I'm some kind of judge or something."

He's wearing a sweater over his open-necked shirt. "It feels strange to be here this way. I don't look the part. I don't feel it, either." He pulls the sweater over his head. "It's hot in here." He sits looking at Marilyn.

Erik is hiding behind a tree. He doesn't want Buford to see him cleaning his testicles. "Don't worry," Celeste reassures him, "I'll protect you."

"Sometimes I wonder if I'm really cut out for medicine. I wonder what I really do want. Have you ever wondered? I mean, if you were to get up right now and go on with life, what would you do with it?"

I don't know, answers Marilyn to herself. *When I figure that out, maybe I will get up.* She stares at the crack in the wall and watches Celeste's gift drip slowly downward, forming large gloppy droplets and then fall to the floor. *When I figure that out, maybe I will get up*, she repeats to herself. *I guess that's the answer.*

"Happy birthday," she says to Christ's eyes.

"Fuck you and the horse you rode in on," responds her savior.

"I don't have a horse. I had a dog once, but he's with you now."

"I know. He's the one licking his scrotum behind the tree."

"That's my brother, Erik."

"I thought your brother's name was Rosie."

"No, that's my dog's name. Do you know where he ran off to?"

"To write some new scriptures."

"Will they tell me what to do with my life?"

"No, but they may tell me how to get down from this damn cross."

"My mother told me you liked it up there."

"Mothers lie."

"Will Rosie tell the truth?"

"Of course not. What good is a scripture that tells the truth?"

"I don't understand," moaned Marilyn.

"Neither do I," Christ answers.

"I wish I understood what the goal is," Buford Abrose sits in his uncomfortable chair and bewails the nature of life. "Why the hell can't we have a script?" There is the slightest flow of tears from his eyes. He pulls out his handkerchief and blows his nose.

Celeste watches carefully to see if he looks at his snot before he puts his handkerchief away. He does. She laughs.

"Why are you laughing?" asks Erik. He tries to extend his tongue like Wang Po's so that he can lick the not too clean linen in Buford's hand.

"Because I'm de meaner," responds Celeste.

"I guess I'd better get home." Buford gets up and starts to pull his sweater back over his head. For a moment he tries to push his head into one of the armholes. Celeste laughs again. "She'll be upset with me if I stay too long," he says as he slumps back into the chair. "No, she won't. I wish she would. She wanted to marry a doctor; that's what her parents told her to do. So now I'm 'the son-in-law failure of a doctor who hasn't given me grandchildren.'" The flow of tears is greater now. Their smell somehow seems different from the years of sweat, urine, feces, blood, snot, and tears that had accumulated in the air of the room.

"God, have pity on me," Buford sobs.

"And fuck you, too, dummy," choruses Christ.

CHAPTER FORTY-TWO

Who will drive out our legions? Who will exorcise our demons? Who will soothe our anxieties? And, who will calm our rages? What music man can lead this motley band? Will we have uniforms – red, marching band uniforms? On that great morning of redemption, will we be spiffy in our new uniforms? Or will we still be mis-draped in our pastiche of hand-me-downs?

At the final coming, will we be the least who are set first? Or will we still be locked up and outside?

One of the chaplains blesses us. He is an oily man. His nose is bulbous and red. He wears a toupee which does not match the fringe of real hair that so badly needs trimming. This has become his vocation – presiding over the services of the damned, going from institution to institution with his tone of falsified piety, blessing the unblessed, promising salvation, saving nothing. He is the charade that ends the charade of a party.

He speaks slowly. He holds his arms extended so that we can see that his hands are manicured and soft. He tells us to go in peace, we who never know peace. He tells us that God loves us, we who feel no love. He tells us that Christ died for us, we who know endless guilt. He tells us that God drives out evil, we who are un-exorcised, we whom the demons of madness are consuming. He tells us that God heals, we who know no health. This is his blessing: that we may know the falsehood of his faith.

Those of us who are free to do so wander back to our overheated wards; the rest are escorted to the same. In this strange unmapped world, these seem two greatly different things.

I arrive at the ward. Bobby is rocking back and forth with each opening of the terror which is a door. He monotones a song of his own creation, "Never share poetry with strangers. They may not know that ice crystals are more beautiful than diamonds, that hummingbirds sing the sweetest songs, that the rainbow is more precious than the gold."

CHAPTER FORTY-THREE

Stan loved Christmas. That our family was Jewish didn't matter. "Chanukah just doesn't have the panache of Christmas," he would say.

Panache was one of his favorite words; he wanted to live in a world with panache.

He loved to sing carols. He knew the words in English, some in German, and even a few in Latin. He loved to find a group of carolers on a frosty Christmas Eve and slip and slide along the icy sidewalks with them. He would sing as lustily as any believer.

Stan loved the grip of winter: the snow, the ice, the steaming breath. What was he thinking going to California? Was that the first hint that he had stopped wanting to live? *Did he think riding his motorcycle into the path of that semi had panache? Is suicide a statement of style?*

We would exchange gifts. As boys, Stan and I would exchange Christmas presents. They were small. Neither of us had the money for large. They had to do with thought more than price, and that gave them great value. I found jazz records and tropical fish for him; he found dog-related gifts for me.

I loved dogs. We didn't have one. My mother considered them dirty, traife. She wouldn't touch dogs or cats or other small domestic animals. In her idiosyncratic theology they were all traife. I obsessed about dogs. I read about them. I collected pictures of them. I fantasized them. I wanted them – kosher or traife, I wanted them. And I was terrified of them.

I was terrified of the ones that chased me as I rode my bicycle. I was terrified of the ones that growled from behind fences. I was terrified of the ones who pulled the leashes taut in their effort to reach me. I was terrified of the ones who lived in other people's homes. Dogs had become my childhood's Holy Grail, filling me with awe, terror, and desire.

The packs of dogs that roamed the grounds of the asylum generate only fear. Dog bites are frequent, especially in the nights. Then, the solitary walker is easy prey for apostate canines that have given up their love of shelter and fire for the fierce independence of the pack. No one has yet died of dog attacks, but many patients and staff members are tooth-scarred. The well-earned delight of a solitary cigarette - that joyous infusion of chemical pleasure and privacy, can turn in a moment's time to a flight to safety or even, perhaps, to pain and terror.

We know where the wild dogs cave: under an unused building, a building that had once housed tuberculin inmates. Its long sleeping-porches are built on now-rotting wood piles. The delicate latticework that had guarded the space under those porches has long since yielded to time leaving entranceways for all manner of beast. Dogs, cats, raccoons, those and more growl at us when we come near. We shout back in mock bravado as we hastily make our way past.

Why did we go so close at all? Because nearby is the path that leads down the steep cliffs to the estuary below. There, at low tide, we can make believe that we are on a country holiday. We can sun and smoke and talk. Sometimes we picnic on candy bars, crackers, sodas, cookies, and other such from the little hospital store. Sometimes we light fires. On occasion, when we are able, we drug ourselves with cheap wine and fire-breathing liquor and then stagger against each other as we climb back up that trail and cling to each other as we lurch past the rumbling growl of that old, deserted building.

CHAPTER FORTY-FOUR

"Slow, slow, quick, quick, quick! Slow, slow, quick, quick, quick!" Mildred's metronome voice droned through the dance music. Mildred was a relative of my mother, of course - a third cousin twice removed or some such. For that reason, I had been given a reduced rate for my ballroom dance lessons. Dance lessons were definitely kosher; in fact, without them, a young boy could only be classified as traife.

They were the key to Bar Mitzvah success – one's own and others'. You could fake the Hebrew, especially the Haftorah, which nobody but the cantor, the rabbi, and the ten old men who prayed together every day knew. You could fake the rocking back and forth and the silent hummed drone of prayer. But without proper dance lessons, you couldn't do your mother proud.

In reality, every child in Mildred's living room had been given the same rate. Each family had been found deserving of its own unique reduction. That was part of her sales technique. She was far better at sales than at teaching dancing; you can always give phony discounts, but you can't teach what you don't know.

"Slow, slow, quick, quick, quick!" Phony, phony, deceit, deceit, deceit! "Slow, slow, quick, quick, quick!" Lie, lie, shit, shit, shit! The mind muddles things. Words become confused. Meanings – where do meanings go?

In the dark recesses of my mind, in the hidden horror of childhood, there, where I do not want to go, that is the home of meaning. Distorted by experience and then again by memory, washed with fear and then again with terror, meaning clings with desperate strength. To what is it clinging? Its roots – such fragile, hair-like roots – hold fast to the images that I cannot control. Like Chia Pets sprouting helplessly fake looking greenery, these images that flood out of my unconscious are covered with meanings. It is only in the groaning pain of sleep that they are revealed. Then they tear at me with the ferocity of wild dogs. My mind is dragged screaming into pain, into memory.

"Quick, quick, slow, slow, slow!" In my dream Mildred's voice repeats and repeats. I see Janice. She watches me intently from the corner of her eye. She is in love with me, as in love as a nine-year-old can be. She writes my name over and over on her schoolbooks. She tells her friends that I'm sooo handsome. Stan and I laugh about her, but secretly – so secretly that I cannot share it even with him – I enjoy the worship. I enjoy the quick, eyes cast down, glances of her affection. I enjoy as an eleven-year-old boy enjoys the new appearance of hair under his arms, around his genitals, on his face and chest. I enjoy the affirmation of manhood.

"Quick, quick, slow, slow, slow!" Mildred pushes me across the room and puts my hands in their proper position. My left hand holds Janice's right. My right hand is on the small of her back. I try to lead. I am not used to leading. The real world does not encourage young boys to lead. I try to push and pull in time to Mildred's metronome. I step on Janice's feet. She steps on mine. We nearly trip and fall. Our bodies are close enough that I can feel the nubs of her not-yet-breasts against me. I imagine that she can feel my penis responding to her. "Quick, quick, slow, slow, slow! Quick, quick, slow, slow, slow!" Life dances on.

In the distorted world of Jewish middleclass deceit that gave birth to Stan and myself, there are the orderly rhythms of foxtrots, waltzes, and cha-chas. The dancers take their mirrored positions, the orchestra starts to play, the Mildreds count, and the world slowly circles the parquet floor.

In the asylum, the dance is chaos itself. Jamul wails the tune, "I just want to talk to you. I won't do you no harm. I just want to know about your different lives on this here people farm. I head some of you got your families living in cages tall and cold." We pirouette in unlikely directions, banging and crashing one into the other. If we dare hold one to the other, it is only for an instant. Then we reel away – away before the rules can strike, before the punishment can come.

CHAPTER FORTY-FIVE

"What do you think?" Buford Abrose asks me. I stare uncomprehendingly. Inmates do not think – not publicly.

He waits. I stare.

He waits some more.

He means well. He must mean well because he has continued to spend these tedious, unproductive hours with me. Weekly, we have met and accomplished nothing. Still he continues.

The winter has given way to spring. Gentle buds are appearing. Evidently, the world will not end this year. Each spring I wait for those buds and wonder if life will renew. So far, life has won out, the buds have appeared, the world has gone on – I'm not sure that is for the best.

"I don't know," I finally offer, afraid to let the silence continue.

"You don't know if you want to go to the circus?" It is half question and half exclamation. His tone implies my stupidity and his frustration.

In truth, I don't know because I don't care. Freaks under the big top and freaks in the asylum: what's the difference? Does it matter?

Tell me where to go, I think, *and I'll be happy to comply. Ask me to choose, and I have no idea. Please, do not ask.*

"It would be fun." He pauses for a moment for that thought to sink into my stone-brain. "Don't you think so?"

"I suppose." My voice is timid, afraid to commit. *Fun,* I think and conjure a world of Chia Pet ideas and mis-ideas. I remember laughter. I remember excitement. They are recalled from far away. Then I remember tears. Wasn't that always the way – tears follow joy as night the day? I feel my eyes misting.

"That's all right," the well-intentioned doctor tells me. "I understand."

What does he understand? I ask myself. I know that he does not, that he cannot. I don't mind. The arrogance of his not knowing puts things back in place. I smile wanly and shake my head up and down. I know that he will interpret my shaking head as he wants, that he will decide for me, that I have once again avoided the terror of free will.

"Did you ever go to the circus when you were a child?" he asks.

Can he not leave me alone? I nod in response.

"What do you remember about it?"

Once again I stare in the helpless numbness that has become my life. Finally, slowly, I speak to my own head. *There was a circus man, whom we once saw, a performer. He balanced on one finger on his electric globe. He spun rings, many rings, while we ooohhed and aaahhed. He loved the trapeze artist's wife, who played the crowd in skimpy dress. I remember his eyes — his eyes wide in lust, even as the circles round his wrist toured a solar system of his creation.*

She wore a blue dress; the spangles shimmered alive. Its light held my eyes captive even as, our mouth engaped, we watched her husband's finale — a cannon launched shooting star who missed his net and fell to death.

To the well-meaning doctor, I answer, "The elephants."

CHAPTER FORTY-SIX

Erik is gnawing on it. He is happy. His tail is wagging, and he is busily gnawing. He had been digging next to the tree for what seemed like days. Now he has it in his mouth. Marilyn recognizes it immediately. "Timmy Wang's wong," she screams. "Drop it, Erik."

But Erik doesn't listen. She recognizes the color and shape of the flesh. She recognizes the scar Timmy Wang had shown her from the day he had tried to zip his pants and caught his foreskin. And she recognizes the scent – still after all this time, the sweet scent of Timmy. "Drop that," she screams again, but Erik drags his prize behind the tree where she cannot see him.

"Do something," she cries to the eyes of Christ.

"There is nothing worth doing."

She remembers the night that the town had driven Timmy and his father, Wang Po, away. They had been tied up and thrown in the back of a truck like animals. Timmy was naked; somebody had pulled the clothes from his young, yellow-skinned body. There was blood running from horrible cuts in the flesh of his back. She had watched in horror as one of the men had sliced his back with a whip. She had screamed out at them, but they had ignored her. They had ignored Wang Po's entreaties, too. One of the men had hit the older man on the head with a bat, and he had slumped down unconscious. That was when they had thrown him into the truck.

She had been surprised that Timmy's wong seemed to enlarge even as he was being beaten. She had wondered if he was enjoying it as they had enjoyed being together. Even now, with Erik gnawing on it behind the tree, Timmy Wang's wong seems larger than life, more vital and real than anything else in her existence.

At last I've found it, she thinks. *No,* she corrects herself, *Erik found it, but at least I know where it is.*

"Isn't that wonderful, Celeste? I know what happened to Timmy's wong."

Celeste is crouched down behind the tree. Marilyn can hear the sound of Celeste's urinating. "Piss on it!" she declares with fervor. "Piss on all of them."

"Master, I have found the secret of true detachment."

The wise man picks up a stick and hits his student in the stomach. As the younger man lays on the ground gasping for breath, he asks, "Why did you do that?"

"To detach you from your detachment."

"I loved Timmy Wang," Marilyn sobs to herself. She knows that love has a way of hurting. "I have suffered so much," she cries.

The eyes of Christ start to laugh. Rosie covers his ears with his paws so that he cannot hear the awful sound of Christ's laughter. "This, then, is the end of the world," says Rosie.

Erik pokes his head out from behind the tree. He still has Timmy Wang's wong in his mouth, but there are now teeth marks all over it. "Can I have some?" asks Marilyn shyly. "Will you share with me?"

Erik brings his prize to the end of the crack. "Eat of this for it is the end of the world," intones Rosie. The laughter of Christ shakes the universe. The marching band is crouched down in a furrow someone has plowed across the field. They are cowering from the awe-filledness of what they are about to witness.

Somewhere on the corridor the janitor is singing. His voice floats like the haunting wail of a banshee across the room, across the scene unfolding before Marilyn. "Take this hammer, carry it to the captain. Take this hammer, carry it to the captain. Take this hammer, carry it to the captain. Tell him I'm gone, Lord, tell him I'm gone."

With all her soul and with all her might, Marilyn reaches for the sacrificial organ, which Erik holds, gently now, in his teeth. Her body does not move. It can no longer obey her commands, but then it has been years since she had last commanded it. Nevertheless, she is aware of a wondrous thing. "And his name shall be Wonderful," choruses the band, who have once again risen to their feet.

Their uniforms are covered with a combination of mud and dung. "If you lie in the farm yard, you'll rise with manure," Rosie pontificates.

"Hallelujah," sings the band marching in place.

"Hallelujah," echoes Wang Po, who is now hanging from the cross from which Christ has climbed down. It seems as if the syllables resonate off his enormous encircling tongue and fill the universe.

That which is the essence of Marilyn slowly rises and moves away from that which appears to be Marilyn. That which is truly Marilyn moves, as if she were the bride of Christ, in a slow, stately march, across the chasm of reality.

Celeste stands beatifically waiting for her friend. Her hand is extended. "If you get there before I do, – Comin' for to carry me home, Just dig a hole and let me through - Comin' for to carry me home. I looked over Jordan and what did I see? – Comin' for to carry me home, A band of angels comin' after me – Comin' for to carry me home."

As that which is truly Marilyn makes her triumphant pilgrimage, the skies shake. There is a darkness gathering over the world, a darkness beyond understanding. Then as she takes her prize from Erik's mouth, the skies open. A torrential rain pelts against the roofs and windows. The flood of water fills the highway and turns the hospital parking lot into a lake. For a few moments, it seems as if the sudden spring storm is going to wash the world clean.

Marilyn holds Timmy Wang's wong in one hand; in the other she clasps the hand of her friend. Marilyn looks upward, and she sees a great wonder – she sees that Jesus weeps.

CHAPTER FORTY-SEVEN

We have gathered by the small store-snack bar that is much the center of our asylum life. This is where we bring our pitiful beggings and the proceeds from washing cars and doing other odd jobs for the staff. A few of the older inmates, those who have some pension or Social Security money, bring that here, too. Inside we can buy little luxuries and those few necessities such as cigarettes, coffee, and soda. Far and away, Dr. Pepper is the preferred beverage of the insane. Coke and Pepsi eat your corporate hearts out.

We have gathered and now we wait. Waiting is something that we do every day – usually for nothing. We have become very good at waiting for nothing. But this day we are waiting for the hospital vans. We are going to the circus. Dressed in what passes for our pathetic finery, we are the weeds of society waiting to infest its lovely middle-class lawn.

Allan has been torn from his post by Marilyn's door. Doris is decked in her full hysteria. Jamul has brought his best invisible guitar. Charlie is ready to go, albeit without his mind, but with plenty of "Oh, boys" at the ready. The freak show is waiting to be populated. We are an easy way to paper the house.

We are waiting for the gray vans with the state logo. The recreation staff finally joins us. They seem even more beige than usual. Perhaps it is in contrast to us, life's colorful castaways. In patient voices they explain once more the rules and policies by which we must abide. Nobody listens. It doesn't matter.

Finally we get to the only topic that interests any of us. Somebody from another building asks about spending money. The question is answered patiently, as tolerantly as if it had not been asked and answered a dozen times before.

We wait longer. Finally, they arrive and we board: Two big vans and two small – thirty passengers plus drivers – three recreation staff, three aides, twenty-four assorted diagnoses, not counting multiple personalities.

Jamul wails for us, "Here he comes, here comes your lover man. Here he comes, here comes your lover man. I gotta get my suitcase and get out of here as fast as I can." Doris bops up and down in her seat. She is out of time with Jamul, but, then, she is out of time with the world.

Bertha, one of the rec workers, starts to sing along. We always laugh at Bertha. Her impulsive nature, her ready physicality, her easy emotion, her unlimited enthusiasm: we see her simple, immediate responsiveness to life and wonder how long it will be before she joins our medicated ranks, the ranks of the diminished capacities. We have nicknamed her BB, Big Bertha, even though she is not particularly heavy. She is named for her gusto not for her size.

Jamul looks at BB and turns up the volume. He reaches over to his invisible amp and turns it up as loud as he can get, as loud as life can be.

Allan covers his ears and starts to rock back and forth. He moans as he rocks. He rocks as he moans.

The driver cannot take it anymore. He yells, "Quiet!" at the top of his voice, a father with unruly children in the back. Jamul wails, Doris bounces, Bertha sings, Allan rocks and moans, and the driver yells. Then the driver turns on the radio. He starts it low; perhaps he hopes we will all try to hear. It just adds to the cacophony. He raises the volume. It feels as if the van will explode. He pushes it to its limit. Jamul wails louder, Bertha sings harder, Doris bounces higher, Allan moans more intensely, the driver yells at the top of his voice, and the radio blares. We arrive at the mall where the giant tent has been pitched.

The pandemonium of the van slowly sorts itself out. By the time we have reached the reserved parking area, we are all sitting in the silent waiting posture of the terrified. Charlie raises his hand, slowly, hesitantly, as he now does everything. "I have to go to the bathroom," he announces. We giggle like his fellow schoolchildren. Bertha signals to an aide, who leads Charlie away.

The aide is hurrying. Charlie can't hurry; he can only shuffle along with the motoric uncertainty of a broken robot.

CHAPTER FORTY-EIGHT

For the better part of a year, Janice and I had stumbled around Mildred's flower-printed living room, listening to her metronome voice and her scratchy records. At the end, we were no more graceful than we had been at the first. Janice had, however, lost her interest in me and no longer practiced writing my name, which made me vaguely sad. In the end, what should have become the fluid joy of movement had become robotic and broken.

The women who dance for the circus have also become non-human. For all their tits, ass, and spangles, they move with little grace or feeling. They have become trained animals. Something of the innate, the natural human has been removed.

The small brass band, metronomed by a bass drum, tries to inspire them. The leader, gesturing almost hysterically, is trying to will them into movement. So, they move – becoming, as they do, ever more out of step. Mercifully, the music stops. They bow. We applaud. They run out of the popcorn and cotton candy infused tent as the elephant sways in. We applaud again. The elephant trumpets and raises his trunk high above his head in what we think is his salute to us the audience. He brings it down on his trainer's head, knocking him unconscious to the dirt-covered asphalt. Then, in full adolescent tush, he attacks the nearest stands.

People scream and run. The elephant trumpets. Circus workers mill about caught in their uncertainty and fear. We, the insane, sit and laugh. Death-defying has become deadly. The circus has lived down to its billing. We sit transfixed while the tent empties around us. The elephant, eventually tranquilized by a man in clown clothes and floppy shoes, lies in the middle of the chaos he has created. Ambulances arrive, and the injured and dead are removed. Still we sit, refusing to leave, refusing to give up the pleasure of the absurd.

Then, his unintentioned baggy pants drooping to the top of his ass, his unbuttoned, florid Hawaiian palm-tree-studded shirt flapping around him, Jamul stands up and starts to scream his Jimi Hendrix lyrics, "Look over yonder, here comes the blues. The thirteenth of anytime, unqualified fools. I can see them comin' wearin' a blue armored coat. He's standin' there with your finest, hittin' wrong notes."

Inspired, Allan climbs up on the bleacher seat, drops his pants and then his bleached to pink mis-washed boxers. He pulls his penis as far upward as it will stretch and starts the excitation of pumping until finally, in a desperate fountain, he spurts his cum into the world.

Bertha, excited beyond the restraint of the keys that she keeps – like any good hospital employee – tucked into her bra, pulls Charlie's head towards her and sticks her tongue deep inside his throat until he gags and coughs in unexpected pleasure. He starts to scream his excitement. "Oh, boy! Oh, boy! Oh, boy!" His voice fills the now void tent.

Doris shimmies her way into position and gives me a lap dance worthy of a New Orleans speakeasy. I, delighted, feel unexpected manhood along with the trepidation of frenzy. I reach up, under her skirt, around the edge of her panties, and feel for the grail that we human apes sanctify with our symbolic lies. Excitement now seizes me, and Doris – now violated, her cock teasing exposed – slaps me hard enough to deflate penis and ego in one withering barrage.

Jamul has changed songs. "I can see my rainbow calling me through the misty breeze of my waterfall." Allan, still pulling at his penis, trumpets in elephantine imitation. Wasn't that a time – a time when madness ruled?

***

Mostly, we sit in exhausted quiet as the vans roll back to the hospital. Only Charlie is still agitated. "Oh, boy! We did it. Oh, boy! We did it," he repeats over and over again in a manic staccato.

"What did we do?" I ask him if only to turn off his endlessness.

"We escaped," he answers with a mist settling into his eyes. "We God-damned escaped."

I pat him on the knee. "We sure did, old-timer," I respond. "We sure did."

Escape is something that happens in the parallel universe of your mind. It is one of those ideas that have meaning, fragile, delicate meaning. Find it for the moment while you can, for it is as ephemeral as the trumpet of an elephant. Here one instant and gone the next. Yet it echoes and reverberates in the vast emptiness of being. Tiny as its roots may be, once watered, it will not desiccate and blow away in the wind of the next moment. Deep in the recesses of my battered mind, the mist over Charlie's vacant eyes gives revivifying irrigation to an idea that has lain dormant. I will – I must escape. I will find that grail, and it will be mine. It must be mine – mine alone – mine to keep.

When? How? These are questions without answers. But I will escape. That I knew. As the vans hurry along the parkway towards our non-home, I turn the idea over and over in my mind. I test it in my mouth as if it were a delicate candy to be savored. I wrap my tongue around it and taste again and again.

CHAPTER FORTY-NINE

Buford Abrose, M.D. is sitting in his tiny office. He stares out the window, watching the pigeons that have nested there strut back and forth cooing to each other and shitting everywhere. The faux balcony has a deep coat of white, and he has often wondered what it would take to return it to its natural dark cement gray. As it is, even on warm days such as this, he doesn't feel that it would be healthy to open the windows and let the breeze-borne parasites in. It has frequently seemed to him that the asylum is a pit of pestilence. Now it feels as if that sense of disease is casting its heavy shadow over his soul.

On Buford's desk is a copy of *The Chronicle*, the local newspaper. It is folded open to page three. "At least," Dr. Lavanger had commented as she handed him the paper, "it's only on the third page, so the whole world won't see it." Somehow, in her mind, he has become responsible for the circus trip, for the crazed elephant, and for the subsequent photographs of Jamul and especially of Allan. It is that photo with its so carefully suggestive blacked out areas – the one that only a laughing god could have posed – that has truly upset her. In the calculus of her mind the dead and maimed are not important. The reality that we might have been killed probably has given her a moment of pleasurable supposition. But that photograph – a photograph that makes our collective insanity visible to the world that tries so hard to deny its and our existence – embarrasses her, and embarrassment is one thing that a supervisor in a state system cannot tolerate. It is the television interview that she does not want to give.

At one level Buford realizes that the whole episode doesn't matter, that people will forget, that nobody is going to be sacked over crazy people acting crazily. On another level, he knows that Susan Lavanger has a long and nasty memory and that her anger might well affect his eventual recommendation. That last is a terrifying thought. He does not want to spend his career in pigeon-shit covered state hospitals, and a bad evaluation by his supervisor might just consign him to such a hell on earth. And, worse yet, consign his unhappy wife with her already dashed expectations to share that hell with him.

Buford knows that he has to speak with each of his patients who had been at the fiasco, to debrief them if he can, and to find some putative therapeutic good in what is clearly a public relations fuck-up.

The small oscillating fan on top of his battered, institutional file cabinet barely moves the stagnant air of the room. It seems to be pressing in on him, constraining his every breath. *I wish I could open those damn windows*, he reflects.

Buford knows that he has to act, to do something that will, if only in appearance, seem to show that he is dealing with the situation; but lethargy has tightened her grip, and he sits staring – staring through dirty windows at strutting pigeons and what must have been years and tons of white bird crap.

***

On the ward, the previous day's exhaustion has given way to a reawakened sense of mad exuberance. Even the patients who had not gone to the circus are talking excitedly about it and questioning those of us who had gone. They want every detail told, retold, and told again. They want to feel that time of freedom, that moment of exaltation that the outside world's moment of chaos had gifted to us. They want to feel that they, too, had escaped into a world in which madness is not a hindrance but a prerequisite for its appreciation and comprehension.

We share. We are not niggardly with the details. If anything, the story grows with the retelling. Voices strengthen. Gestures intensify. Not surprisingly, the greatest attention on the ward goes to Allan. Along with the other details, his penis grows in the iteration and reiteration of the tale. He becomes the talisman of the ward, the hero of the hour.

As determined as we inmates are to revel in our story, the staff is equally determined to make an end of it. They watch with eagle eyes for any infractions that might justify a shot of Valium or the use of restraints. They are warriors, sentinels, on guard – protecting the gates of sanity lest it be invaded by the germs of our derangement.

Give the inmates of an asylum a sense of freedom and you set their wildest fantasies into full flight. Even those whose brains had been excised, whose madness had been lobotomized, whose energy had been convulsively zapped, even they can feel the agitation of such freedom. Bedlam is close at hand, and we are all enjoying its coming – we are all listening for the angelic trumpeting of the leviathan that will tear down those walls and set us free. We are all ready for the hallelujah morning. "Free at last! Free at last! Great God Almighty, I'm free at last."

Only, we aren't free. There are no trumpets. There is no invasion. The walls still stand, and gradually, even as we rejoice, they are closing back around us – pushing us into our proper shuffling roles, into our hesitant, dependant stature. In the warmth of those pigeon-cooing spring days, we soon realize that we have gained nothing, that desire alone does not make you free. Excitement gives way to frustration. And, in its turn, frustration gives way to anger until the ward is awash with it.

Yet isn't it true that the journey of a thousand miles starts with a single frustration?

CHAPTER FIFTY

Is it a moon-struck sea, this madness on which we bob about? Are we, unknown voyagers on the Titanic, heading each of us for our truck, our chrome chair, our elephant in tush? Whatever the cyclic forces that drive our world, catatonic as she is, Marilyn still cannot avoid the tides of emotion that rise and fall in the ward.

Marilyn knows that she knows so much. She has never understood why other people don't know what she knows. On the other hand, there are always so many things she doesn't understand. That was what she had liked so much about playing bumperpool with Timmy Wang. They had both known and they had both not understood.

Rosie knows, too. But he understands. He understands because he had understood about Erik. It is strange how Rosie knows about the things you can't talk about because there are no words, at least not words you are supposed to use or are only supposed to use at special times. At Christmas Marilyn had been allowed to mention Erik. On August 18 she could mention him, too; but then everybody cried. They didn't cry at Christmas. They had a ritual. "We all miss him. Some things are in God's hands."

Rosie always mentions Erik, but he never uses the words that Marilyn's parents could hear, the words which they would not allow. Rosie had missed Erik and wanted to dig the thing that looked like Erik up from under the tree so they could take it to a wizard who could make it become Erik again. Rosie was sure in his tail wagging dog way that they could find the wizard, but Marilyn didn't believe Rosie. After all, she hadn't been able to find Timmy Wang.

"Timmy Wang" was another of the words that she wasn't allowed to use — not ever. He wasn't supposed to have died. He was supposed to have disintegrated, disappeared, been blown away into forgottenness. Marilyn had been very careful to talk with Rosie about Timmy Wang when her father hadn't been around. Rosie didn't want to help find Timmy Wang. He liked sniffing at Marilyn and didn't want to share her with Timmy Wang's wong.

It had been an accident that they had met in the crack opposite Marilyn's bed. Rosie was playing with Erik. They were rolling on the ground. Erik threw a stick and said, "Fetch." But Rosie had jumped up and down and wagged his tail so that his whole body wagged with it. When he had jumped very high, he had landed on a branch, which was where Timmy Wang had been hiding.

Marilyn doesn't know where Timmy Wang's father, Wang Po, had gone. She has never asked Timmy. It doesn't seem like something she should ask. After all, what if Wang Po had gone to the world of dead people? Erik had gone there, too, but he had been able to come back to throw sticks for Rosie to ignore. Maybe Wang Po hadn't found the way out.

Marilyn wondered if she could help find that doorway. She had asked Erik to help her, but he had told her that everybody had to find it for herself. That had seemed like an awfully grown up thing for Erik to say.

"Where did you learn to say something so grown up?" Marilyn had asked.

Erik didn't answer. He threw another stick for Rosie who was jumping up and down. Timmy Wang hadn't said anything either.

"When the saints go marching in, when the saints go marching in, I want to be playing the numbers when the saints go marching in."

There is a marching band going across the field where Erik and Rosie aren't playing fetch. "Watch out," Marilyn yells as if she were really saying things and they were really listening. She can feel her heart racing as she sees the band getting ready to step on Erik and Rosie.

"March, march, march, the boys are marching."

"No, it's June, and you didn't say 'may I.'"

"April fool." Erik pulls his head out of his body and bounces it like a ball of shit. Rosie likes that game. He sits with his own head cocked to one side watching.

"Do we die?" Marilyn asks.

Through the crack Celeste answers, "If we want to." Her voice is calm and ressured.

Erik says, "Never."

Rosie says, "Arf," which wasn't what he really meant but he couldn't think of anything profound to reassure himself. So he figured if he couldn't say anything meaningful about it, maybe he shouldn't say anything at all. And, when you get right down to it, "Arf" is about as meaningless a thing to say as "Thou shall not commit adultery," or "Thou shall not kill," or "Thou shall have no other gods before me."

Timmy Wang is far too busy playing with his pool cue to say anything, which is probably a good thing, too. The best advice he could give Marilyn is to die right away and to come play bumperpool, and Marilyn knows that she really must be able to move in order to die.

The band is marching in the other direction. They are playing a special song. Marilyn knows it is special because she cannot hear it. She thinks, *You never can hear the important things.*

She wonders what her mother might have to say about death. Her mother had never talked about it, not even when the cancer worms were eating her. When her mother died, Marilyn had wished that someone would say something about death that made sense; but instead everyone told her that she wouldn't understand. And, of course, she hadn't.

"From ashes to ashes, from dust to dust," the minister had said. He was wearing the funny collar that hid his Adam's apple.

Marilyn wondered why he thought her mother was made of ashes and dust. She knew what her mother had been made of. She knew but she couldn't say the words. They were the words of power. Those were the words that upset people. She had to be very careful what words she said.

"I miss my mommy," she had said. Everybody gathered around her and told her it would be all right. She had known that they were lying. "Where is she?" she asked, trying hard to say what everybody wanted her to say, knowing that meant saying nothing.

"She's with God. She was very sick, and God took her to be with Him so she wouldn't be sick anymore. That's how much He loved her."

If he loved her so much, why didn't he just keep her not sick? she had asked herself. She knew that it would never have done for her to ask that question aloud.

That night, when she had been left alone, when she was lying in bed with Rosie by her side, she turned to him and whispered into his ear. "Flouxbine," she said, and he had whined in agreement.

CHAPTER FIFTY-ONE

The day has worried on.

It gnaws at Buford Abrose, who sits hour after pointless hour trying to make sense of the circus catastrophe, trying to get us, his patients, to make sense out of an elephant's madness and a voyeur turned exhibitionist.

It gnaws at me as I stare at the flickering, rolling television and try to plan – to plan a real escape, to plan a real freedom.

It gnaws at Bobby who holds himself firm to a doorframe in safe retreat from earthquakes. "Hold tight your dreams," he sings in his off-key monotone. "Don't let the clowns steal your floppy shoes."

It gnaws at Charlie, who paces and agitates into the air. His machine gun "Oh, boys" rattle through the day and into the relative quiet of the night – night lit by the weary glow of flickering bulbs – until he ends up with a butt full of Valium and the obscene silence of a room with padded walls and floor.

In another ward, in another building, it also gnaws at Jamul, our young chocolate pudding of a musician. He is a volcano ready to spring into eruption. Under the surface, his magma is superheating. The very core of him is expanding and forcing its way to the surface. This night he will lead two of his peers to freedom. Like his ancestors, he will follow The Drinking Gourd until he has arrived at freedom. He can feel the spirit stirring within – the spirit of the oppressed, the spirit of the enslaved, the spirit of the asylumed.

***

Jamul has spent most of his life in the hospital, but nobody could have given a good reason why – a bad reason, yes, but not a good one. He had been brought by his parents, black father and white mother, at the age of four. The attending physician had noted his incoherent speech and disturbed gait and balance; he had also noted a cyanotic blue tinge to Jamul's lips. The parents professed that while they loved their son, he was beyond their attempts at management. In those days, that was all it took – a parental throwing of their collective hands into the air, a custodial "we surrender." Jamul was hospitalized for observation with a tentative diagnosis of neurological dysfunction – a lovely catchall – or schizophrenia – a universal category.

Jamul seemed to improve quickly. His parents were called and told to take him home. "You said he had either a neurological condition or schizophrenia," said his father.

"Neither of those is curable," said his mother.

"So either you mislabeled him and have committed malpractice, or you're wrong now and are committing malpractice," they both said. "We ain't taking him. You keep him."

The doctors, stymied by their own fears and visions of lawsuits, send Jamul back to the wards. His parents disappeared, never to return. Letters were sent. They came back unopened.

A caseworker was dispatched. She learned that the parents divorced shortly after Jamul had been hospitalized and had gone their separate, unremarked ways.

"They were constantly fighting," said one neighbor.

"If they didn't have the kid, they would have split right off," said another.

The hospital administration considered going to court to terminate the parents' rights and then placing Jamul for adoption. One problem: who'd adopt a five or six year old black kid with a history of psychiatric hospitalization? The answer was obvious. In the service of mercy, Jamul had stayed officially crazy.

He had stayed put until forty hours after the elephant. It seems only proper to date events from the moment that the pachyderm raised his trunk in trumpeted protest. At forty hours, Jamul lets himself and two other young patients out the window of his dormitory. Every patient who had wanted to could have learned that trick. You take a piece of wire coat hanger, bend a little cloverleaf in it, and insert it in the lock of one of the metal screens. Turn slightly, and freedom beckons.

Carefully putting his air guitar through the window ahead of himself, Jamul shimmies out the up-window and, holding on to the pigeon-crudded ledge, drops to the ground. The other two boys follow him. A fourth patient, who is always too willing to cooperate with everyone, closes the window and the screen behind them. The three escapees make for the woods. They duck and weave and laugh and shove and push.

Stealth is intended but totally unnecessary. Night staff being what they are, nobody notices their elopement until the next morning. Even then, there is no sense of urgency or alarm. It is assumed that the three will return when they get hungry. Lunchtime passes, and still no teens. The local police are finally notified. About four in the morning, one of the three is hitchhiking on the expressway. A state police car happens on him, and the troopers soon have him back at the hospital.

"I don't know where they are," is his response to being questioned about Jamul and the third boy. Tired and hungry, he is given a bologna sandwich, a pill, a glass of milk, and sent to take a nap. Nobody has noticed the blood on his clothes. When you are a castoff in castoffs, nobody wants to look at you, to notice your appearance, to notice your existence.

The third member of the little posse comes back to the hospital on his own. Late that night, he climbs one of the leaders and raps at a bedroom window. That it is a women's bedroom alters nothing. A makeshift key is procured and the screen opened. The boy makes his stealthy way to his own bed where he awakens the next morning trying to make believe that he has been there all along.

Another day passes. Still no Jamul! Throughout the hospital we begin to wonder if he can, in fact, make his way to freedom. Is it possible that he will never return?

***

Because he is under eighteen, the hospital has to pursue Jamul's absence. If he had been passed that landmark birthday, he would have been free to elope, free to manumit himself, free to face the impossible task of surviving with no education, no skills, and no social network. As it is, the police dutifully come back five days after the elephant. They take the first of the two other boys, Glenn, into an empty office and ask him about their escape. Glenn talks about a shack that they had found. It was something that a gang of town kids had created – there, far from supervision, they could smoke their weed and drink their beer. It wasn't much, Glenn explained, but it was where they had spent the first night.

In a fit of self-righteous energy, one of the cops asks Glenn to show them to the shack.

"I can't," he responds. "It burned down."

"How come?"

"Tommy and I torched it."

"How come?"

"To hide the evidence."

"The evidence of what?" asks the cop, now more interested.

"What happened to Jamul."

"Which was?"

"He got killed."

"How did that happen?"

"Tommy hit him up the side of his head with a cinder block."

"Why would he do that?"

"'Cause he wanted to play Jamul's guitar, and he wouldn't let 'im."

"What happened to the guitar?"

"When we see'd he wasn't breathin' we threwed it into the shack and burned the place."

They handcuff Glenn and tell him to lead the way to what remains of the shack. In the cinders and ash they find what remains of Jamul's body. The wild dog pack had found him and had eaten his well-barbequed flesh. They had gnawed on his bones and dragged them about. Only the hospital's dental records will confirm his identity. The quiet of the hospital, the absence of his wailing sounds, will confirm his death.

***

They bury that which remained of Jamul on a chilly spring morning. The priest, looking distracted and uncaring, rushes through the rite of burial – pauses only long enough to cross himself and say "Amen" before scurrying to more important duties, a meeting with the hospital's administration.

With the decline in hospital population there has been some discussion of closing the interfaith chapel, and the chaplains have arranged a meeting with the hospital director and two members of the board of overseers. The hospital administrators are planning to offer a new chapel located in one of the still operating buildings. If events follow their typical course, the chaplains will at first decline. The administration will up the ante by making extensive renovations. The renovations involved will probably cost the state four times the annual cost of maintaining the present chapel. The chaplains, feeling that they have accomplished something, will agree. Two years later that building will most likely be closed, and the administration, concerned that the hospital not appear to have neglected its patients' souls, will reopen the chapel, which will then require extensive restoration funds. So goes the state; so goes the world of sanity.

"I take it the boy was Catholic," another resident comments to Buford.

"I guess so, the priest claimed his body." He does not know how ironically appropriate that statement is, how many times the same priest had claimed Jamul's body in life. It could only be prayed by those who did know that this priestly man might soon be incarcerated in another asylum, one in which he might become the prey. He is truly to be scorned this man of God. Male and female, young and old, willing and resisting: he has abused all in a true embodiment of the polymorphous perverse.

But this day, at this moment, the priest is far more concerned with the material status of faith within the hospital. So he hurries through the burial service without any personal words, and there is nobody to object. Susan Lavanger has insisted that all her psychiatric residents attend as part of their training. They have formed an uncomfortable knot, most already preoccupied with creating insights to share at their next grand rounds, internally cursing their supervisor for making a meaningless death so seemingly real.

The only mourner of free choice is the janitor who works the building where Jamul has lived for the past five years. The janitor, a state-employee lifer as trapped in the world of the asylum as Jamul had been, stands beside Buford Abrose at the hurried service. He would in time die and be buried in a town cemetery only marginally better kept than the hospital's. When the priest has left, the janitor says, "It doesn't seem right that someone should leave this world without music." He starts to sing "Nearer My God To Thee;" Buford tries with limited success to follow along.

When the hymn is finished, they turn and start to walk across the rough field which separates the cemetery from the hospital road. The other residents and Dr. Lavanger are already well ahead. "Why did you come?" Buford asks.

"I figured it wasn't right. Nobody should go out of this world alone. Besides, he was a good enough kid – never caused me no extra work."

They walk in silence for a moment. "Oh, when the saints," the janitor sings.

"Oh, when the saints," echoes Buford.

"When the saints come marching in," sings the janitor.

"Oh, I want to be in that number, when the saints go marching in," they sing together.

Straining to listen, Buford hears a strange music echoing in the background. It sounds like an electric guitar playing along with the two men.

"When the new world is revealed, I want to be in that number when the new world is revealed."

***

As their last notes echo among the brick buildings and fade into the void that now and forever holds Jamul, Buford can hear my well-amplified air guitar. I am not so talented as my young friend had been. My voice is neither as loud nor as strident. I can only stumble through words that I have just partially learned. But my heart is honest. "It's too bad, Lord, my brother can't be here today. It's too bad my brother can't be here today."

***

Nurse Teraso has decreed that no patients are to attend Jamul's funeral. It is standard procedure; death might be too upsetting. So we have gathered by the entry to the hospital and are leaning against the wall that Jamul had held in place so many Sundays. We keen our sadness into the chilly morning breeze. We stand well after the point when the residents have dispersed to their various rounds, well after the point when the meeting between chaplains and administration has ended, well after the point when the janitor has finally gone home.

We stand and we mourn until it is time for dinner. Then, hungry and tired and knowing that there is no use in remaining, we turn back to our lives. I do not know how many of us are envying Jamul, but I'm sure that some are wishing for their own freedom, even if it is the freedom of clammy earth over a cheap fiberboard coffin.

As the sad quiet of evening settles itself over the brick and cement of the asylum, as the moon tosses about in a whirling sea of clouds, as the faint odor of lilac and roses wafts from the town's gardens, I sit by a window that looks onto a circle of weeds and scrubby bushes – a reminder of better times for the Department of Mental Health – and think about my own freedom. To end where Jamul has ended, to end without having achieved meaning, this seems more terrifying than all the perils of life.

I swear to myself, "I will survive. I will be free. I will live." It is a sacred oath.

In the background I can hear Charlie's rat-a-tat voice, "Oh, boy! Oh, boy! Oh, boy! Oh…"

CHAPTER FIFTY-TWO

Reaching the ward, Buford looks back on the stairways fenced in black metal and locked gates. Unconsciously, he caresses the large key in his hand, the one that has opened each of those gates in turn and which will now open the ward door. Opening that last barrier, he starts to walk down the hallway toward the nurses' station. The nurse with the seductive ass is again on duty, and a part of him wants to talk with her. *Maybe she could understand*, he muses.

Instead, he turns into Marilyn's room. There are two maintenance men hard at work. One man is plastering the crack in the wall; the other is busy repainting in the same hideous color. He looks up when Buford comes in. "I can't remember the last time that we did maintenance on a one-patient room. You know how the state is – a major job or no job."

Buford nods and shrugs his shoulders to indicate the bewilderment of the state system. "We're going to repaint the entire room, though," the second man reassures. "It will be in good shape for her."

"That's fine," Buford responds reflexively. "Where is she now?"

"They have her in the dayroom. She'll have to sleep in one of the dormitories tonight. We wouldn't want the fumes to cause any brain damage." He laughs at his little, insensitive joke.

"No, we wouldn't," Buford responds with a hint of feeling. He looks at the last small stretch of crack yet to be spackled. Beyond the crack he senses some movement. "They're going to wall up a cockroach," he thinks to himself. Then he squints to look more carefully. He rubs his eyes to remove the hallucination and looks again. Still he sees them.

They are gathered around a tree. He recognizes Marilyn immediately. The second woman he vaguely recalls having seen when he had first visited the hospital for an interview. The naked, hairy boy is like nobody and nothing he has ever seen: he is the essence of the feral. Neither has he ever seen a dog holding a pen and writing in a giant ledger. They are having a picnic. At some level of his being, Buford realizes that they are feasting on manna, manna in the shape of a giant penis. They are passing it around, taking turns gnawing at it, but with each bite it replenishes itself.

The last of the spackle fills the crack, and Buford can see no more.

He does not want to see more. Shaken, Buford can only assume that he has been affected by the chemicals the two men had mentioned. To believe the evidence of his eyes, to accept his vision as reality, that would have meant the existence of something beyond reason or, alternatively, madness. He stands in the hall to compose himself and takes some deep breaths to drive the fumes from his lungs. Then, he walks briskly, as if to assure himself that he is in control, into the dayroom to see how Marilyn is faring. *Or, perhaps*, he thinks, *the word should be fearing*.

Strapped securely into her chair, she is sitting against a wall. There is a window to her left. Through the steel mesh screen, he can see a robin sitting patiently in her nest waiting for her eggs to hatch. He can see only the slightest edge of delicate blue poking itself from beneath her. He wonders if the babies within will survive. It surprises him that after putting up with the pigeons outside his office, he can still care about a bird's survival. Indeed, it seems somewhat unreal to him that he can still care about anything, especially something as fragile as the mind of this woman strapped into her chair.

Allan is sitting next to Marilyn, holding her hand, and speaking softly to her of how beautiful her room will look when the maintenance men have finished. She doesn't respond. She doesn't touch him. Her hand is like soft clay being molded by his. He smiles at her and makes believe that she smiles back.

Buford decides not to interrupt. Instead, he goes over to the nurses' station and spends a few moments idly flirting with the nurse whose ass he so admires. *I wish we could make babies, too*, he thinks. It is unclear if the nurse or his wife is the other half of that we.

To hide his intent from himself, Buford pulls a BIC from his shirt pocket and writes a couple of unnecessary orders on charts. As he puts the cheap plastic pen back, he wonders where he has left his expensive gold pen. It is once again in his drawer, once again under his underwear, but in his mind it has vanished – along with any fantasy of a private practice, of someday having wealthy patients and countryclub memberships. Somehow, somewhere, over the past weeks all that has become lost to him. He hasn't mentioned the pen to Alice. There is no point in aggravating her over something that really isn't that important. Besides, hadn't he been intending to give it up for five-and-ten BICs long before?

CHAPTER FIFTY-THREE

This night I have dreamt of long lumbering freight trains making their tortured snaked ways across great plains and over towering mountains. They cross mighty cascading rivers and small, tranquil streams. They passed through tall-standing forests and cut through fields of crops ready for the harvest and others waiting to be sown. Those locomotives with their seemingly endless burdens are seeing a world that I have never seen. In slow, stately passage they bisect the cities and towns that compose a world that I have never visited.

There is one crossing where the gate remains forever down. The bells clang, and the red light flashes. Waiting patiently behind it is a truck, a semi, large and powerful, a monster of the roads. Held safely by my unconscious, it will not derail the train. It will kill no one this night. In my dream I think this, and I see Stan, unchanged by time, smiling at me. He is high above. There among the clouds, there by the moon, there with the mythical beings that people the stars, my cousin rides his motorcycle in heavenly bliss.

If only we lived in dreams and our suffering was really the stuff of sleep, I think, *then death would truly have no dominion.* But I know better, and awake to my own tears, to my own terror, to my own sense of helpless loss.

***

Poor Marilyn, trapped uncomprehending in a strange bed, in a strange room, surrounded by the snores and yelps of other women, women whom she does not know, whom she does not want to know. Still, she sleeps. She has no choice. The nurse has given her more than enough medication to assure her sleep. Then one of the male aides, one whose fancies are the sickest, whose desires are the most primitive, gives her more. So she sleeps. She sleeps through her fear, through her loneliness, through her rape.

The next morning, it is hard to wake her. The aide who tries pulls back the bedclothes and reveals blood – blood from the cruel lacerations of her vagina – lacerations and wounds of unnecessary roughness, of rapine will at its most animalistic. So, still somnolent, Marilyn is taken to the medical unit where she is inexpertly treated. No one thinks to call the police, for no one wants them here. No one thinks to collect evidence of rape. No one thinks. In the asylum, the crazy do not merit thought.

The sperm making their way through her uterus don't think either. They do what sperm do: they search for eggs to fertilize, for life, however merited or not, to begin. They find one just exiting its fallopian tube. It is sex at first contact. Conception. What more can be said? Deep inside a catatonic a new being is coming into being. What terrors it would experience, what end it might reach, what evils it might do, what asylums it might people: those things are yet to be written. It is enough for nature to know that conception has occurred.

When the moon has waxed and waned nine times, when the cold of winter has returned to the asylum, when the robins have flown south, when the cold rain once more cracks against the windowpanes, then life will commence. That is nature's plan. She needs no other.

***

In his rented house near the hospital grounds, Buford Abrose tries to hug his wife, to pull her to him and inspire her to love and to inspire himself to feeling. She pulls away. "I have a headache," she moans as she so often has over the recent course of their marriage. Her headaches had started when they learned that she was barren. What a horrible word the gynecologist had used to describe her! It conjured a field of rocks and dirt, a world bereft of even the hint of green. Still, it was a word he could not escape. In its grip the little warmth that remained between them had turned cool. In its grip she had turned to pains of the head to cover the pains of her heart.

Perhaps if the rest of their marriage had been happier, if Buford had not seemed such a failure, she could have recovered at least some of her feelings. But a wasteland within a wasteland is not a place for anyone's recovery.

Buford wonders how long their marriage can survive. He knows that a divorce during his residency would look bad, but he isn't sure to whom. He knows that he would be forced to discuss it at grand rounds – that thought alone makes him slightly nauseated. He knows that he wants to hold on until he has become board certified, until he holds a piece of paper that means he has a right to carry the keys of power to write the prescriptions of control.

He also knows that he still wants to love his wife and that he still wants her to respond when he pulls her into his embrace. He wonders if adoption would work to free her from the psychological barrenness that has become so much worse to live with than the physical. But deep inside he knows that if she were not barren, Alice would leave him – perhaps she would have already left. And if she did, he is not sure it would matter.

Only the thought of being alone scares him. Again, he tries to pull her closer.

She resists more forcefully. "I told you I have a headache," she moans.

"I just want to hold you."

"Not tonight." She rolls over as if to try to sleep.

Buford gives up. He stares at the black ceiling and thinks of the robins' nest, of the eggs waiting to hatch, of the life within.

***

The eggs are never to yield life. They are, instead, a feral cat's dinner. Would there have been live babies? That nobody can tell. Given the levels of poison used by the state to protect its property against flies, tics, mosquitoes, given the spraying done by men too foolish to mask their own mouths and noses as they gape skyward at the stream of cream-colored death that arcs from their hands, it is chance as to what can and what cannot survive.

Nor will the feral cat survive. Protecting her own young, responding to the demands of instinct, she will die amidst a pack of dogs. Her kits, too, will die. Their flesh will join Jamul's. Like his, their bones will be snapped in search of marrow. The dogs will also die. Animal control will eventually trap some and poison the rest. That will happen in the future after a visiting child will be viciously mauled. She will not die, but she will be horribly scarred – both outside and in. The trauma will eventually contribute to her madness, a madness that will finally complete the circle when she sits staring into space on an asylum ward.

The debate over the survival of the fetus growing inside Marilyn rages for weeks. The hospital is her legal guardian, which means that the politics of abortion are not to be ignored. Most of the medical staff urge an abortion on the grounds that the pregnancy might complicate Marilyn's condition. Nobody is quite sure how a catatonic state could be compromised for the worse, but that is their position. Quietly, they talk about the impossibility of placing the infant for adoption. Who would take the offspring of a schizophrenic and a brute capable of raping her? The hospital director pushes the decision up the food chain to the state office of mental health. The state director refers the problem to the

171

governor's office. The governor weighs in on the side of the most vocal and coordinated voting block in the state – the right to life community.

At the hospital there is consternation. Secretly, Buford Abrose rejoices. Were it up to him, he and his wife would have volunteered to take the baby. It is not up to him. His wife is horrified at the thought. "Have you been having an affair with her?" she demands to know.

Buford offers to take her to see Marilyn, to see the absurdity for herself. She cries and refuses. In his terror of her leaving he begs. She becomes angry and refuses. He gives up. She stays angry. It is, after all, a good way to avoid sex – sex that would make her feel even worse than she already does. To have been outdone by a catatonic seems far more than she can bear.

Their marriage will linger, held together by the threads of mutual disappointment and fear of letting go, but it has died just as surely as new life has begun to flutter inside Marilyn.

CHAPTER FIFTY-FOUR

Marilyn's world has changed in ways beyond imagining. As new life takes root within, the lens through which she has lived, through which she has visited her reality, has been closed, spackled, and painted. No longer can she see those who have been so very important to her. No longer can she speak with them. No longer can she seek their council and learn their wisdom. Celeste is gone. Rosie is gone. Erik is gone. Timmy Wang is gone. Her brass band is gone. And, most assuredly, Jesus is gone. She no longer has a choice. She has no place else to turn, no other world to enter. She does the only thing left to her. When she is three months pregnant and the governor has ruled out an abortion. When Buford's wife has taken to falling asleep on their rented threadbare couch in their rented house. When summer has started to turn orange and brown. When the wind again carries the chill of winter.

One morning, when Buford comes to see her, when he has settled himself in his chair, a pen at the ready to doodle away the hour, when he says, as he has so many other days, "How are you feeling today, Marilyn?" she looks towards him and answers. "I think it's time for the vacation to end."

And so it is. It is time for Marilyn to face the world that assails all of us, to give up the hope that there will be – that there could be – some better world hidden inside the wall, scurrying about within our vision, within our eyeshot, but far from the prying ears and eyes of our neighbors.

She arises that morning from the bed that has been her home for days, months, years. She does not sit in a geri-chair. She does not need to be strapped in place. She showers as a normal person would, shuddering at the filth of the hospital's bathrooms. She eats as a normal person would, raising and lowering the over-sized spoon into the mush of cereal and chewing on the cold, burnt toast. She brushes her own teeth and wipes her own ass. She puts on a dress that has been worn by many others, but she puts it on her own body with her own hands.

It is, for Buford and for the rest of the staff, a day of triumph. For Marilyn it is a day of resignation. Having no choice, she will, as befits our humanity, her humanity, survive.

***

Alan is ecstatic. He has, in the full force of his lunacy, decided that he is deeply in love with Marilyn. That she had never responded to his attentions, or, for that matter, to anything else, only makes her seem the more tempting and forbidden. While he would never have admitted it to the staff or to Marilyn, he is convinced that he and he alone has impregnated her. When fantasy becomes reality, all things are possible. When love has become enchantment, does it not give life its creation?

Being a gallant and gentlemanly individual, albeit a voyeur and, more recently, an exhibitionist, he proposes marriage. True to form, he does so with his penis hanging out of his pants, which earns him two hours in seclusion. One of the aides, Mike Farragut by name, now to be rechristened Little Man, has taken a great offence to Alan's exhibitionism. We, the male patients, had all decided that it is because of Alan's prodigious size – size sure to make normal men feel inadequate.

No sooner is Alan released from his straightjacket then he reappears in Marilyn's room to press his suit. There are those who want to believe that Marilyn's miraculous recovery has been complete. They are taken aback when she says yes to her crazed suitor. The rest of us simply nod our heads in time to the spheres that rule the universe and laugh at the ridiculous notion that the once crazy are somehow less mad simply because they have escaped one set of symptoms. Actually, isn't everybody mad – the patients, the staff, the visitors, the people randomly passing the asylum on a day's outing? Why, then, should Marilyn have done otherwise?

They ask the priest who had buried Jamul to perform the service. He refuses. They ask the protestant chaplain. She refuses. They even ask the Jewish chaplain. He says yes if they are both Jewish and they contribute to the building fund. They settle for the judge of the local traffic court. He squirms a bit at the idea, but when pushed he admits that he has no right to deny his services simply because the couple are mad, a position he buttresses by referencing his own son, whose marriage has been a disaster, but whose sanity has never been questioned by anyone except his parents.

It is a happy affair attended by all who can get day passes and a handful of staff. Since the happy groom cannot get a day pass as he had recently masturbated in the middle of the little snack bar/store and then, to make matters more revolting, had mixed his cum into a soda – Doctor Pepper of course, which he then drank – proclaiming it in drawn-out suggestive syllables "innviggorraating," Alan has to be accompanied by a staff member. Bertha, ever excitable, volunteers her somewhat questionable presence. If only there could have been an elephant in attendance, it would have been a lovely affair.

After the vows, we go back to the ward for ice cream, sheet cake, and fruit punch – nothing half-carbohydrate in that place.

Bobby has waited for us rocking and pill-rolling by the ward door, his body pushed into the shadow of its frame. He rocks and pill-rolls and sings. "There is smoke that brings tears: the smoke of love, the smoke of letting go. There is sorrow that brings laughter: the sorrow of love, the sorrow of letting go."

It is in a way a double party. We are celebrating both that morning's wedding and my freedom.

I have, against the advice of the staff, who feel that I am no longer prepared to deal with the outside world – a feeling supported by the twelve years I have already spent at the hospital – handed the hospital administrator the requisite letter of intent, the one that says that I no longer feel that I need custodial care. The staff have objected, but they cannot prove that I am any more dangerous to myself or others than the average guy, so I am free. I am free to leave my little nest, my psychological womb. I am free to come and go. I am free to face life – to succeed or to fail. God, help me, the fragile egg has hatched. I am free at last.

The hospital has rounded up a battered cardboard suitcase and a variety of hand-me-down clothes. The staff have dug deep into their own pockets to help me get started. They present me with twenty-six dollars and eighty-four cents – a fortune within the asylum grounds but nothing once outside.

With that, a last helping of cake, a few ungainly embraces, and a chorus of good lucks, I walk out of the building. At the foot of the front steps, I look back at the door that is already closed against the chill of November. I pull my jacket close around me, and start walking. I walk the three hundred forty-seven paces to the road. I count them as I walk. I keep my eyes focused straight ahead, and I count. I don't dare to look around until I have finished number three hundred forty-seven. Then I know. Then I am sure. They are not coming after me. I am not sure if I should feel relief or terror. Some small part of me has been hoping that somebody, anybody, would stop me, that they would find a reason to stick a syringe of Valium into my butt and drag me into that nice, safe, padded room.

But it isn't to be. I am free.

I have no place to go and almost no money with which to get there. But I am free.

I have no job skills and no employment history. But I am free.

I have no relatives, at least none who would want me reemerging into their lives. But I am free.

I haven't thought past this moment. I had told them that I had, but I haven't for a simple reason. I could not have imagined what this moment would be like. And I certainly could not have imagined beyond this moment. I still cannot.

CHAPTER FIFTY-FIVE

I walk through the brick entry, out into the world, onto the asphalt of reality. As I pass through the phalanx of inmates who have gathered to see someone – anyone – actually leave – not in an ambulance or a state van but on his own feet in his own time through the front gate, as I manumit myself, a thrilling and fearful thing of which they can only dream, my peers do not cheer or applaud. No, they stomp their feet in time with my steps and share in the sense of my exodus.

One youngster, whom I had seen once or twice hanging out with Jamul smoking a fag and sharing a secret, comes over to me and offers his hand. It is so unexpected that at first I hold back. Then I reach out to shake it. But that had not been his goal. He hands me a piece of paper. "This is from Jamul," he whispers. "Read it after you're out."

I stick the paper into one of my ragged pockets. "Sure," I respond in an uncertain voice.

"Please," he urges more strongly, "read it. For Jamul. From Jamul. Please."

I nod. "I'll read it."

He smiles, pulls away, turns around, and walks back, slowly shuffling back towards the waiting brick building.

Later, when I am alone, standing at the Greyhound and waiting for a bus to carry me off, I pull it from my pocket.

It is a tattered paper, unlined, misspelled, written in childish block print that rollercoasts. It is a poem.

There's this word I've heard – freedom.
I'm not sure what it means.
One thing that I'm sure of is
it don't belong to me.
Not inside these walls of brick
with Haldol holding me.

I may be one dumb nigger,
I may be one damn fool,
but I know that if I stay here
I never will be free.

They locked me up a child,
and I never went to school.

I've been sheltered from the world.
I guess that I'm naïve.
But I know I've got to run away
if I'm ever to be free.

I may be one dumb nigger,
I may be one damn fool,
but I know that if I stay here
I never will be free.

I play the air guitar.
I try to make believe.
But the music in my soul
makes me want to leave.
Someday I hope, outside of here,
my music will be real.
I'll tell the world about the things
these folks have done to me.
I'll tell them of my hopes and dreams.
I'll tell that I'm free.

I may be one dumb nigger,
I may be one damn fool,
but I know that if I stay here
I never will be free.

And if I never make it,
and if I die a slave,
if they keep me down
until I'm in my grave,
I hope someone listens
to my voice upon the wind;
I hope they'll hear my story
and think what could have been
if only someone cared to free
all the slaves like me.

I may be one dumb nigger,
I may be one damn fool,
but I know that if I stay here

I never will be free.

CHAPTER FIFTY-SIX

I should have started earlier. I'm too old, and it's too damn late. I wish that I could blame someone else for my mistake. But it is mine, and I am stuck with it. I think about turning back. Lots of times I think about it, but I don't do it. Instead I wander. I wander the country. I wander and, in my way, I marvel.

Now, I've heard lots of descriptions of this country. I've heard about waving plains beyond the eye's reach. I've heard about mountains that tower until their snowy peaks hide in the clouds. I've heard about verdant forests and massive cities. I've heard about wildflower moments of solitude and crowds that carry a person along. I've heard about the ribbons of macadam and the singing steel tracks. I've heard about the mighty rivers. I've heard about the great swamps and the water-stingy deserts. I've heard about the great vault of blue sky and the thunderheads with their cooling rain.

Oh, there are lots of great descriptions to be heard, and I've heard them. But they haven't been my experience. It's hard to notice the wonders when you're trying to figure out how to get your next pack of butts and your next cup of coffee. That's what I've run on for all these miles: coffee and cigarettes, the All-American jag.

What have I seen? Mostly dirty dishes. Grease encrusted, long-since stained dishes, and mugs tinted the color of the millions of cups of joe that they've held. I've seen the dishes in Chinese restaurants. Boy, have I seen Chinese garbage! I've plunged my hands into it and into hot water. Water so hot that my skin puckered on contact and for so long that my hands can no longer feel heat.

I've washed a lifetime of dishes in a week and then washed more. Greasy spoons in the middle of nowhere and diners set near to highways: they all have dirty dishes. And they all have cans for garbage to hoist and carry when full and then to clean when empty. And they always seem to need another poor sap, another itinerant, another wayfaring stranger to do that dirty work.

Then there have been boxes: boxes full of a thousand things, boxes being hiked on to and off of trucks, boxes being loaded into cellars, boxes being delivered to third story walk-ups. There have been boxes to teach my muscles – my long hospital softened muscles – how to work, how to suffer, how to feel pain, how to sweat, how to grow strong in their weariness.

Day laborer that I am, I haven't seen a nation's majesty. I have seen its dirt, and I have eaten its crumbs. I sleep in rooms that stink of smoke, beer, and cheap sex. They have cigarette burned furniture and windows with cracks that have been taped and taped again. They have beds that creak and moan with mattresses made of rocks and quicksand, mattresses that defy sleep until my body is so used that it can no longer stay awake. Yet, for all their horror, many – most – of those rooms have come with a Bible. A Gideon Bible. Who needs it? When you're living from dump to dump, from handout to handout, from backbreaking day job to backbreaking day job, God seems mighty far away. You don't have much interest in lying in bed and reading the Bible. You don't have much interest in reading anything. Although, I will admit, that an occasional piece of porn, left by a past visitor and overlooked by what passed for housekeeping, would hold my attention long enough for a bit of self-pleasure, for a moment of cherished escape.

I am sitting in one of those drab rooms set in the middle of a main street gone to shit in a Texas town that had once raised cattle and then oil but had finally given way to a Wal-Mart and then to poverty. After a day of painting an old water tower, with my shoulders so sunburned that I cannot sit still, I have bought a pad of yellow paper and a mechanical pencil and started to write. I have started to write this story, the story of my life in the asylum, of what I have learned and of what I have not. I write because it keeps my mind off my shoulders and the indigestion of one too many greasy burgers and God knows how many, too many, cups of coffee.

I write with vividness of memory that cannot be erased. I write with purpose, and yet I know that I make naught but markings in the sand.

CHAPTER FIFTY-SEVEN

The glare of the late afternoon has relieved.

Now a sliver moon floats above the lavender and apricot sunset. As the moon rises in the sky, the pastels of its birth give way to a gasp of blood orange and then to darkness. Shadows of mountains stand menacing sentry against the eternal darkness of night as I step down from the semi that picked me fresh from another hash house in Socorro to the sudden oppressive heat of Phoenix.

"Sorry," the driver says with a shake of his droop-lid head, "far as I can take you."

"'Preciate it." I clip the words.

He nods and lets off the clutch. The semi moves on, leaving me in a cough of diesel.

Another city, another fleabag, another shit job. I shrug, pick up the taped and tied suitcase, and walked towards the "ote" with its three remaining orange sticks of a sign.

Phoenix, I think. *No new beginnings here. No redemption, but...* I stop to scratch an itch that is burning my balls. *But no memories either*.

I walk up the two cement steps, open the dirt-tinted door, and walk into the lobby. It is shabby, reminiscent of a hospital dayroom, yet clinging with tobacco smoke intensity to a past of leather chair gentility and six-gun solemnity.

Another city, another hotel, another shit job – for another while. I walk, not quite sure, towards the old front desk with its oak pigeon-holed case holding heavy keys and a few slips of paper.

The clerk's stare takes in my shabbiness, and I can see his distaste.

"I'd like a room," I say even though I am a few steps away. "Nothing too expensive, just a room, for the night." I know my voice sounds weak, still the inmate's, still filled with pleading and dependency.

I mov closer and know that he wants to pull back. I take out my wallet. He sees it and relaxes ever so little. It isn't a welcome, but a reluctant acceptance of a paying customer.

The elevator works its noisy way to the fourth floor. Marred, scarred, and smelling of poisoned souls, it is a dim foreshadowing of the room to come. The corridor into which it lets me is an alleyway of chipped doors and flickering fixtures. The odors of food, sweat, and sex – especially sex – fill my head. I wish myself somewhere, anywhere. But here I am.

My room, as worn-out and exhausted as I, as dingy as my prospects, looks out through torn curtains and smoke slicked window onto a street, a small parking lot, a convenience store – in which I know I will find the strong coffee, pre-made ham and cheese sandwiches, and candy bar that have become the supper of my wanderings.

It is sad. I am depressed. Part of me wants to cry. I have escaped one asylum for another – another place of loneliness and failure.

Still, there is exaltation – the exaltation of freedom – the joy of choice.

Tomorrow will come: that shit job, possibly another even more run-down hotel, a lonely wandering of friendless streets, often a desperate six-pack of cheap coolers. Tomorrow will come and another after that, each ending in the ghostly shadows of impending defeat and yet each, too, containing the possibility of something better, of something however fragile rising from momentary glory, from a lavender and apricot moment of joy. And I will seek it. I will continue – westward, toward my unfinished business, my pilgrimage. And then, who could know? Towards the promise, the promise of lavender and apricot, to the promise of freedoms yet unknown.

CHAPTER FIFTY-EIGHT

I have kept working, and I have kept moving. Since I don't have any place to go, I go everywhere. I have lost myself in the world, and I am surely lost to it. Occasionally, I think of sending a postcard to the asylum, if only to make believe that I am anchored somewhere in the world. I wonder: If Marilyn's baby has been born? Was it a boy or girl? Is it crazy yet? Can the mad lovebirds survive? I think about sending a postcard, and it goes unsent. In Omaha, I went so far as to look for a card with a nice picture, but I used the money to buy another pack of butts. You have to prioritize in life.

Most of my transportation has been by thumb. Mostly, truck drivers pick me up. Glad for some company, they pull their rigs to the side and slow just enough for me to hop onto the running board and get a good hold on the handle before they start moving out. I clamber inside, breathless and grateful, with my lungs full of diesel smoke. They'd greet me with one of those stock questions: "Goin' far?" "Where ya headed?" "Where ya from?"

Things could get quite chilly if I didn't pretend that I had some purpose, some direction. Answers like, "I'm just drifting," and "it doesn't matter," don't go over too well with these hardworking jockeys of the road. They are all about destinations and routes, about making time and miles, about schedules and money. Pretty soon I realized that I needed to have a story at the ready. I needed to have a reason for being on their road, for riding in their cab.

I figured out that I needed to be anchored at one end or the other. I could be from Gypsy, Maryland trying to see America, or I could be from back east trying to get to Gypsy, California. One end or the other, I had to have some place that defined me – the guy from Gypsy or the guy going to Gypsy, it didn't matter. So I picked my destination, the only destination that meant anything to me. Outside of the hospital the only damn place in the world that meant something to me.

It is this scenic overlook to the side of a highway in the Sierra Madres. High in the mountains of California; here is the spot, the beautiful spot where Stan had parked his bike and waited. Not once but twice he had waited. He had waited for death, for the ultimate concrete reality. I became a pilgrim. Truck drivers have looked at me with respect when I told them my mission. They have even asked one another if they were going my way. If anything, they were too damned helpful. Since I have no idea what to do next, I haven't in any great hurry to find this overlook.

Once I got to the right general area, it took some real searching. I had to find newspaper stories from a long time back, stories that told about his death. They were sad stories made sadder by the fact that they were lies – lies about a tragic accident. But they were the stories that I needed. I followed their lead, and I found this lovely spot. That part of the stories was true enough – this is one hell of a spot.

Now I'm sitting here and thinking about my cousin. He'd always said that he wanted to see the world. I figured meant getting away from his home, from its rage and sadness. He'd bought that bike and rode it all over the country. I wonder if he washed dishes in some of the same holes that I've worked. Did he see the beauty they talk about or the shit that I've lived? I guess I'll never know.

Stan was a good guy. That much I do know. He wanted to live in a good world so I guess it's just as well that he didn't live too long.

There isn't any kind of memorial, nothing to mark Stan's death. The blood is long gone from the asphalt. The last bits of his flesh have long been eaten by crows or scavenged by insects. He is gone. His soul, if such a thing exists at all, is far from this place – far from this place of beautiful sadness. I hope….

Report of Highway Incident
Trooper Geoffrey Adams

Dispatch notified me of a traffic accident at Scenic Stop 28 on the Old Mountain Highway. I found a rental vehicle driven by one Walter Smith of Cincinnati, Ohio. Mr. Smith said that he has been on vacation and that he and a woman named Bertha, who has been staying at the same hotel, decided to take a drive into the mountains. When they had seen the signs for a scenic overlook, they decided to pull off the road to engage in some physical intimacies. As they were pulling into the lot, the woman became quite excited. She reached down with her left hand and started to open Mr. Smith's pants. Evidently, her actions so excited and distracted the driver that he stepped on the accelerator instead of the brakes. The car lurched forward hitting an itinerant, whose name I have not been able to learn. The man was launched over the protective stonewall, on which he had apparently been sitting and peacefully writing. His body is somewhere below the site. Presumably a search team will have to be sent to recover it. At this time, I am in possession of the yellow pad on which he was writing and his battered cardboard suitcase, which contains some rather old and worn clothes.

In my opinion, this was a tragic accident, and no charges should be filed against Mr. Smith or against his passenger if she should be located.

AUTHOR'S NOTE

This novel has been a long time in the birthing, over forty-five years. It is dedicated to my cousin Herb, who died in the hills outside of Los Angeles many years ago. He was my childhood best friend, and his death still affects me.

Then there are the other people whose lives have helped shape these pages. Many of them were at one time or another my clients. Some I met working in a state hospital; others were clinic or private clients. I hope I did them decent service then, and I hope that these pages also do them a service by making readers aware of the pain that fills so many lives.

I want to mention those who have helped bring this book to publication. There are my editors, Cha Tori, whose skill with language was more than matched by sensitivity to the characters he was helping to bring to life, and Deb Harris, who has kept me directed to those pesky details of grammar and verb tense. Thanks to my wife, Roz, who has read, listened, and discussed endlessly. I also appreciate those who have heard me read portions of this book and encouraged me to bring it to completion.

I hope that you have enjoyed reading Memoirs From the Asylum and that it has made you think and feel.

Sailors should be bold:

lean into the wind,
hold fast to the lines,
fly on whistled prayer
as your fate designs.
Taut the canvas pulls
the small craft to heel.
To adventure bound –
with excitement feel.
Fast the current flows;
pray the ropes will hold.
as the tempest blows.
Sailors should be bold
while the world they roam
every port a home.

About the Author

A New Englander by upbringing and inclination, Ken Weene's career – primarily in New York – included teaching, pastoral care, and psychology. Throughout his career Ken has also been devoted to writing. His poetry has appeared in a number of publications – both in print and on the web. He has authored a number of professional publications. His short stories and essays have also been published. One of his short plays was recently workshopped. An anthology of Ken's work, *Songs For My Father*, was published 2002.

Memoirs From the Asylum is Ken's second novel. *Widow's Walk*, also from All Things That Matter Press, was published in 2009.

Ken and his wife, Roz, now live in greater Phoenix where he spends much of his time writing.

ALL THINGS THAT MATTER PRESS ™

FOR MORE INFORMATION ON TITLES AVAILABLE FROM
ALL THINGS THAT MATTER PRESS, GO TO
http://allthingsthatmatterpress.com
or contact us at
allthingsthatmatterpress@gmail.com

www.ingramcontent.com/pod-product-compliance
Lightning Source LLC
Chambersburg PA
CBHW031111260626
47172CB00001B/314